Having reached the protective shadows of the Fox Den, Lukos and Kit barely have time to breathe before their pursuers pick up their trail once more.

Only now, an evil from eras past has been awakened and released to hunt them, creating panic in the world underneath Limbo.

Meanwhile, in the city itself, forces of nature and political masterminds begin to clash, forming alliances and making bargains that even a devil would hesitate to agree to.

A sacrifice will be made, but it may be too little, too late.

Hollow World

The Thief's Sacrifice

HOLLOW WORLD

The Thief's Sacrifice

C. Michael McGannon

Hollow World:
The Thief's Sacrifice

Written by C. Michael McGannon

Cover Illustrations by Rainey Leigh

Cover Layout by Matthew D. Smith

Published by Incendia Books, 2016
An imprint of The McGannon Group, Ltd. Co.

Hollow World: The Thief's Sacrifice / by C. Michael McGannon—1st Ed.

Summary: Lukos and Kit continue to run from O'Toole and his forces, taking refuge with the eccentric Mr. Tom's Fox Den, which is threatened by their presence

1   2   3   4   6   5   7   8   9

ISBN-13: 978-0-9861458-9-6

www.IncendiaBooks.com

PART 2

"I could tell you my adventures—beginning from this morning," said Alice a little timidly: "but it's no use going back to yesterday, because I was a different person then."
– Alice's Adventures in Wonderland

Chapter 6: Flee into Hell

Tom Vix's eyes narrowed and he shook his head, leaning forward on his walking stick. He grasped the metal fox head tighter, pricking his finger on one of its tiny metal teeth.

Kit did not deserve his anger. *How could she know how important this lowly servant boy is? How could she know that his presence could overturn everything that we've built underneath Limbo?* He allowed his thoughts to check his emotions.

Across the cavern, Lukos followed Kit around like a lost automaton mutt. Which, as far as Mr. Tom was concerned, wasn't too far from the truth.

"Dammit, girl. Of all the places to stick your nose . . ."

Pan ran up to him, young eyes dancing with the water's flames. "Jimmerson finished tying everything down. We're ready."

Mr. Tom tapped his cane against the rock. "All right, then. Let's go."

The Fox Den mobilized, children marching and scrambling among the shadows with their backpacks, steam carts crawling over the rough cavern floor. It was a surprisingly quiet procession, but for the chugging and hissing of the carts. It was because of the relative silence that the metal *Thud!* sent Lukos' heart racing.

The entire Den came to a halt. More metallic sounds — clanks, thuds, clicking — scrambled to reach them from the large sewage pipe they were passing beneath.

Mr. Tom whistled and the Fox Den scurried into action. Their carts were pushed into a shady area and covered with tarps that matched the cavernous terrain, and then the children hid behind pillars, between cracks, and nestled into crevices that Lukos hadn't even noticed. A hard yank pulled Lukos under one of the carts and its tarp. He stifled a pained hiss as the bullet wound in his side shifted. Kit hushed him, raising the tarp just enough for them to watch from below. With a crash, an access hatch in the pipe flew open and a filthy bronze Hollow leapt from the hole. It was unnerving to behold—like a humanoid frog, but with no face, only teeth. Lukos recognized this design. It was one that had never been put into production, as its horrible visage was found to be too much for the general public.

Looks like the nobles moved ahead with the production anyway, thought Lukos, *only not for Limbo's streets.*

Four smallish arms stroked the ground, grating, as the Hollow lifted its head and sniffed the air. With a low growl, it spun toward the hidden carts, back legs tensing, pistons pumping, ready to jump. From somewhere above, Lukos watched as a young man jumped onto the Hollow, wielding a gun and a thick bamboo stick in his hands. Beside Lukos, Kit's body went rigid. "Pan!"

The brave figure struggled to stay on the Hollow's back, with the vile machine bucking and snarling beneath him. The weapon that Pan brandished was only a grappling gun, which he fired, lodging the hook into a large stalagmite, wrapping the cord around the Hollow. As he attempted to jump off, Pan stuffed the bamboo into the Hollow's snapping maw before being flung toward the carts. Lukos realized what the bamboo was at the same time the Hollow Man realized what Pan had done. It was an explosive device, and the Hollow reared in violence, throwing out its arms, giant teeth chittering. *BOOM!* The cavern shook as smoke burst forth from the Hollow's seams, covering the scene. *Whatever was inside controlling that monster couldn't have survived*, Lukos thought to himself.

Beside him, he couldn't help but notice how Kit's eyes were rapt, searching. The smoke began to clear, revealing the strung up Hollow, hanging limp against the rope, smoke still flowing from its gaping mouth. It was a testament to the metals the nobles used to construct the Hollows that the thing was still in one piece.

Pan emerged from the carts, hair tousled, wiping grime from his cheek. "Damn thing." He sidestepped one of the Hollow's arms — the creature was still alive, weak, but reaching for Pan. The low growls it emanated disturbed

Lukos, but not as much as the smoky black tongues that wriggled out between its teeth. Pan jeered at the Hollow, dancing just out of its reach.

A couple of children ran from their hiding places to crowd the young hero, jumping up and down.

"Pan, that was magnificent!"

"Great job!"

"You killed it, you beat the frog!"

Pan waved them aside, "Didn't kill it enough, apparently."

"Everyone get a move on!" Mr. Tom yelled, limping into sight. "No doubt they heard that explosion. Hollows will be here soon. Jimmerson, get those carts rolling!"

A strong looking woman named Joanne and a slim, lithe woman named Vasi rounded the children back up with help from David and Star, setting the large group in motion again.

Kit slid out from underneath their cart slowly, eyes on Pan, who himself quickly noticed her. Lukos didn't like the way their eyes met, feeling heat prickle across his shoulders. He said nothing and followed Kit as she stepped closer.

"I thought you were dead," she whispered.

Pan leapt forward, sweeping Kit up in a hug and spinning her around. "You did come back! I had trouble believing the old man." He set her on her feet. "I knew you'd find your way home one day."

Kit caught her breath, giving Pan a sad smile. "It's not like that. I'm leaving. This is Lukos."

Lukos stepped forward, reaching for a handshake, which Pan eyed with suspicion.

"Mr. Tom told me about you, too." Pan seemed to study Lukos for a minute before returning the handshake, squeezing a little too hard. "So you're the one who finally got Kit in too far for her own good. How'd you manage that?"

The nobles, the Hollows, the Rusted Rose burning, people dying . . . too much had happened, and Lukos couldn't think of a single thing to say. The Hollow continued to growl and grasp at the air.

"Lukos, this is Pan," Kit finally interjected.

Pan looked at her. "A real talker, this one. Come on, we can catch up on the way to the hole." He helped get the steam carts back into motion, and the procession began again. A *THUD* from above stopped the Fox Den once more. Silence, but for the quiet chug of the carts.

At the head of the line, Mr. Tom held up a gloved hand. From the same pipe that the Hollow had appeared, there came the sloshing sound of footsteps. Slow, relaxed. Every second step sounded metallic, banging against the metal pipe. *Thud, clang. Thud, clang. Thud, clang.*

Mr. Tom's face drained of its color. He started issuing the children forward and grabbed two men by the shoulders, heading to the back of the line.

"What's going on?" Pan whispered.

Mr. Tom grasped his shoulder, fingers digging in as the footsteps drew closer. "I need you to lead them. We'll distract him, you keep moving. Get as far as you can, quickly."

"Him who?"

Thud, clang. Thud, clang.

"LaCrucis."

Everyone seized at the name. Lukos had no idea who they spoke of, but their visible fear bothered him.

Pan shook his head. "I'm coming wi—"

"Shut up!" Mr. Tom tapped his walking stick on the ground twice. "Don't be an idiot. I need you to take care of the Den, Pan."

Thud.

"Okay." Pan shook himself, "Okay. Come on, Kit, help me get the little ones going faster."

Clang.

Lukos watched as the parties separated, the three men hurrying past the sewage pipe's open hatch, Kit and Pan pushing members of the Den over a peaking incline as they rushed to the front. He followed, throwing glances over his shoulder as the *thud, clang* neared the open hole.

"Lukos!" hissed Kit. "Don't dally!"

The last of the steam carts crested the incline, disappearing from sight. Lukos hurried, looking over his shoulder one last time.

The man called LaCrucis stepped out of the sewage pipe, landing solidly on the cavern ground. He was long and lean, face hidden under a wide-brimmed leather hat. A mottled leather duster with a high collar hid the rest of his body, except for the large mechanical piece that was his right arm, and his steam-chugging left leg.

LaCrucis crouched next to the still squirming Hollow, then slammed his right arm into the thing's mouth with all the force of a piston. The creature inside screamed as black smoke poured from within.

"Lukos, get down!" Kit demanded.

LaCrucis' head snapped up, two glowing white eyes blazing themselves into Lukos' mind. He stood up with a violence that made the Hollow Men look kind, and Lukos froze with fear.

Mr. Tom and his men appeared from behind the stalagmites, shooting LaCrucis in the back. The monster stumbled, then whipped around, drawing a large pistol outfitted with a bayonet the size of a cruciform sword, firing back at the men. He raised his bulky right arm, a cannon blast ringing out. Smoke mushroomed from the arm, obscuring the scene.

Kit yanked Lukos down as the attempted ambush continued.

"I'm sorry," he said, the image of those eyes still burning through his skull. "I-I didn't know."

"Just hurry." The fear lingered in her voice as well.

Another gunshot echoed in their ears, followed by the scream of one of Mr. Tom's men.

The group moved as quickly as the steam carts allowed. Some of the teenagers in the group—their eyes world-weary and hard—suggested that the younger children be escorted ahead, others staying behind with the carts to catch up later.

"No," said Pan. "I don't think splitting the group any more than we already have is a good idea."

Lukos felt worse underground than he had on the streets. True, they had been patched up well. Lukos' bullet wound had been disinfected, sown up, and rewrapped, while Kit's leg had been discovered to have been twisted badly, but not broken. She wore a makeshift brace to help lessen the pain of walking. Still, they were missing hours of sleep, and neither had eaten a full meal in some time.

The atmosphere wasn't much better. There were

onlookers in the streets of Limbo, with alleys and doors, passages to escape through, and nooks to find shelter. Underneath Limbo, there was only this expansive cavern. Tunnels that Hollows could appear from at any second surrounded them, and a forest of bulbous stalagmites and rocks ruptured everywhere, while machines in the background sang and whirred, giving voice to his every fear. They had simply traded the despair of the people for the emptiness of the underworld. It was at once vast and claustrophobic. Lukos ducked under a mass of wires that seemed to appear and disappear into the darkness of the cavern ceiling.

"Who, or what, was that?" Lukos finally asked.

Kit's answer was quiet. She searched the dark constantly. "That was LaCrucis."

"A Hollow?"

"Worse. No one really knows what LaCrucis is. Well . . . Mr. Tom knows, but he won't talk about it. LaCrucis has always been more of a scary bedtime story than anything else. If the nobles woke him up . . ." She stopped looking around, eyes drilling into Lukos. "Why do they want you back so much? You have to know something, Lukos."

He remained silent, digging through his own heart and mind for an answer that he didn't have.

Kit limped forward, leaving Lukos behind to catch up with Pan. He watched the two from a distance, feeling alone.

Pan looked at her, his gaze lingering. "There you are. I was wondering if you were going to spend the entire trip at the back of the line. You know, you could still stay," he said when she didn't answer.

"I can't."

"One day we're going to overthrow the nobles, Kit. Your face won't always be on a wanted poster." He tossed his thumb toward Lukos. "In fact, once we get rid of Lukos —"

"You're not going to end their rule in your lifetime, Pan. Not down here hiding and running in circles. Mr. Tom might have filled your head with glory, but his war days are over. Can't you see he's too old and tired?"

"So you'd rather go outside the wall?"

Kit shrugged sadly. "Dead in Limbo, dead outside Limbo. What's the difference? At least my death might be quick outside the wall."

"That's not funny Kit."

"And who's to say we don't make it?"

"Who, you and Mr. Weak but Silent back there?"

"Close your trap. Lukos is a good man."

Pan snorted. "A good man relying on a street thief to survive, who would've been dead or worse if it weren't for her. Limbo's best street thief," he added fondly.

"He's stronger than you think."

The two fell quiet, fuming to themselves for a moment. It didn't take long for Pan's mischievous smile to return. "Just like old times, huh? Don't you miss it?"

Despite herself, Kit smiled. "Sometimes. It is nice not to have to argue every moment of every day. But at the same time, I have missed you."

Pan wrapped an arm around her shoulder. "Think it over at least, okay? I know Mr. Tom isn't going to lead the

Fox Den in a war against the nobles. But you and I could do it. We could do anything together."

Kit wiggled out from underneath his arm, catching a nervous glance at Lukos over her shoulder. "I'll think about it."

Oil, sour sweat, and smoke swirled to make Industrial's signature aroma. The figure in the alley took in a long whiff, finding pleasure in the air's miserable perfume. He waited, watching foot traffic from behind green tinted glasses. More smells—mainly booze and grease—filtered through the constantly opening door to The Saint and The Dragon, a seedy bar crowded in close to the edge of the district.

Mammon pulled out his gold pocket watch. He grew impatient, his time a valuable resource.

Finally a smallish man, crooked and lean, limped out of the bar. The man wore a threadbare beanie drawn down to his eyebrows, working hard to cover a scraggly mop of curls. The man spotted Mammon from across the street, instantly and visibly nervous. He crossed the cobbles, dodging a sickly horse and buggy.

Mammon addressed him first. "Mr. Allwurst?"

The man nodded. "They just call me Allwurst, sir."

"You're late," Mammon hissed.

"Sorry, sir."

"Do not be late again. Time is of the essence right now. Do you know where they will be?"

The vagabond swallowed before speaking, his throat dry. "There are a few possibilities."

Through gritted teeth, "You said you could find them."

"I can! I can, sir, don't you worry."

"Good. Remember, no one touches the runaway."

Mammon handed the frightened Allwurst a black satchel. The man struggled for a moment under its weight. Taking a look inside, he saw the gold bricks, and on top a beautifully crafted long pistol.

"Try not to get caught on the streets with that. I'm sure anyone in Industrial would kill for the money alone, not to mention the firearm."

Allwurt's lips stretched over his crooked, incomplete set of teeth. "You forget, sir, I was a member of the Fox Den once. Finer set of criminals there never was. I know how to take care of myself."

"*Hmph*. See that you do."

Allwurst stepped back across the street, a new malice to his posture. Mammon doubted the man would live to enjoy his new fortune, but he would fulfill his purpose.

An Avidum Hollow lurked on a shaded wall farther back in the alley, clicking forward at Mammon's gesture. He signaled for the creature to follow Allwurst — find his home, his hovels.

He wanted his gold back when the man was dead.

Chapter 7: Of Teeth and Promises

The sighs and coughs of machinery grew louder over the course of their journey, and flashing lights soon joined the audible incursions. Its gray metal blending in with the cavern's landscape, a filthy recycling station slowly became evident. It nestled into the forest of stalagmites, a platform built underneath to compensate for the cavern floor, which sloped to the now distant Lake of Fire. Huge pipes pumped into the station, water and other materials sloshing in. A couple of cranes with oversized hooks hung static over the station, sludge and debris hanging from their long arms.

Jimmerson and Daniels checked their weapons, other adults following suit. Vasi and Joanne ran up to the station and hauled open a huge metal door.

"Keep your eyes open and be aware everyone!" Pan yelled, his voice carrying just above the noise. He smiled at the children, who grinned back, putting on brave faces.

Inside was hot and sticky, with a stale, pungent odor that caused Lukos to gag. Old tech ran loud, requiring little attention, echoing off the vast walls and metal support columns. The four large waterwheels that spread across the right side of the building croaked and groaned as they turned, keeping the machines running.

Even locked away from the world outside of Doyle's estate as he had been for so many years, Lukos recognized the waterwheels and pumps for what they were — relics from the pre-war era. Simple, practical, sturdy. A few electric instruments still glowed with life, others having burned out long ago, but the station didn't seem to rely on them.

Lukos thought about asking what the station was for, but Kit was far ahead and he felt silly asking the children, who were on high alert. He studied the machines, trying to discern their purpose when he spotted a large vat. Waste and sewage slunk from overhead ducts, plopping into the vile water, and other conduits led from the vat farther into the station. Looking deeper into the dark, he saw several other containers of the same design.

He'd always known that the water in Limbo was to an extent, recycled. It was clean, running through complex bioalchemic purifiers. Still, it twisted his stomach to be reminded where the water flowed to and was ultimately delivered from. He tried to focus instead on their situation and the imminent threat at their backs, though the constant rushing of water and discordant machines made it hard to gather his thoughts. Massaging the back of his neck, Lukos picked up his pace to catch up with Pan and Kit.

"Who takes care of the systems down here?" he asked, trying to strike up a conversation.

Pan laughed. The sound of water seemed to grow louder in Lukos' ears as they passed the last of the vats. The end was in sight—a rusty door that had long since fallen off its hinges.

"No one comes down here," Kit explained.

"O'Toole comes down here," said Pan, sounding seri-ous. "Him and his monsters."

"Ash. She's one of them." Kit's face grew pained. "She's

not human.”

“I heard. Damn O’Toole and all of his wretched puppets. I’m sorry, Kit. I know you thought she was a good friend. We all did.”

“That’s what we get for trusting people.”

“People outside of the Den,” he corrected.

Lukos watched as an unspoken tension grew between the two.

“Come on! When did you lose your faith in the Den, Kit?”

“Shut up, Pan.”

“People come, people go, people die. It’s not your fault, and it’s not Mr. Tom’s fault either.”

“Shouldn’t we be keeping an eye out for Hollows?” Kit snapped.

“Is that why you’re sticking with him?” Pan asked, voice rising as he pointed at Lukos. “You think you have to save someone now? Keep them alive or something?”

“You watch what you—”

“HOLLOWS!”

The bellowed warning from Daniels caused Kit and

Pan to both stop talking and spin, looking for their pursuers. Two of the frog-like Hollow Men came into view, their great leaps closing the distance faster and faster. The children started to panic and cry.

"Everyone! Keep going!" Pan yelled over the noise. "We can block them off in the hallways! Joanne, how much bamboo dynamite do we have left?"

"After your stunt earlier? Forty-two," the woman yelled in reply. "We're already short by eight, the smugglers are expecting—"

"We can deal with their expectations later!"

Joanne nodded, setting fire to a couple of the explosives, dropping them, and ushering everyone past. The Fox Den crossed a railed, metal bridge, passing over one of the ditches that powered the waterwheels. Two loud booms shook the bridge, but the Den didn't hesitate, quickly pouring into the broken doorway.

"In the hallway!" cried Pan. "We can close them off here!"

It was a tight fit with the carts. There was hardly any light until Joanne lit a lantern, although Lukos immediately wished she hadn't. A Hollow was already in the dark hallway, its big metal teeth stretched with an anticipating grin. It moved slow, deliberate . . . a predator with guaranteed prey.

Behind the group came a low growl. The other two Hollows had caught up, their shells singed from the explosives, but otherwise unharmed. Giant teeth chattered with the prospect of their prize.

The Fox Den was closed in. Their escape through the narrow hallway had become their trap, and everyone knew it. The adults quickly moved to the fringes, keeping the children toward the middle — a hopeful gesture in the middle of certain death. Without asking or hesitating, Joanne pulled out another stick, striking the fuse.

The Hollows charged — fast, hungry. Men tried pushing the Hollows back with guns or large pipes that they could get their hands on, the metal objects being quickly crushed and swallowed. The younger children cowered into a tighter ball, knowing their defenders would not be able to protect them for long.

Joanne jumped in front of the single Hollow in the hallway, thrusting her arm down its gullet. Without hesitation the creature bit down hard with a *crunch*. Joanne screamed, but only pushed herself forward, her arm disappearing up to her shoulder. With another gnash of the teeth and a slight tug, the Hollow ripped her arm away. Blood splashed the front of its carapace. It seemed to laugh at her, and then its body shuddered with a *BOOM*. Tongues of fire flicked from its mouth and exhaust pipes as the creature crumpled, its limbs reaching for purchase in the hallway. As before, black tendril-like tongues leaked from between its teeth, moving slow.

"Choke on that, you bastard!" Joanne turned around to face the Den. She already had two more bamboo explosives in her remaining hand. "Pan, go! Take the Den out of here. No questions. I'll take care of the other two."

Pan steeled himself and nodded, giving the woman an embrace. "All right!" he yelled, his voice impassioned. "Let's move forward people!"

With terror in their eyes, the children of the Fox Den ran, following Pan and Kit beyond the dying Hollow. Lukos looked back to see one of the men being viciously chewed to death as Joanne, holding two explosives in one hand, shuffled toward the two Hollows. She was bleeding out fast.

Those at the end of the Fox Den saw her coming and knew what was about to happen. They scrambled, catching up with the rest of the group, a hardened sadness in their eyes.

This was life to them, Lukos realized. This was day to day survival. He turned his head away and put one foot in front of the other. He could feel his mind going numb, but he couldn't stop here.

Alone with the two Hollows and the remnants of the body they devoured, Joanne dropped one of the bombs at their feet. The other, with her remaining hand, she freely placed in one Hollows Man's mouth. They left the dead body, gleeful to cause pain to someone else still alive.

Several moments later, flames filled the hallway following a loud explosion. Lukos flinched, the shaking warehouse snapped him out of his shock. Ahead, Pan paused for a moment, looking over his shoulder.

Kit kept moving, head down, turning another corner

of the hallway.

Smoke filled their nostrils as a large hole in the wall leading to the outside came into view. There was a collective release of tension from the Fox Den with the end in sight, and then a scream from behind them quelled what little hope they had. A small girl had been caught by a Hollow. Its shell coated with grime and ash from the explosion, the monster snapped its jaws menacingly at her face. Several members of the Den began firing, trying to distract the thing.

Lukos knew their guns would not be able to stop the Hollow Man. Close to the tail of the group, he ran to her, knowing this could very well be the end for him. But he couldn't live with himself, watching another person—another small child—die if he could help it. Maybe she could at least escape.

Somewhere behind him, Kit was calling for him to stop.

Lukos had never been a fighter. Not physically speaking. But growing up in Doyle's estate had not been a simple existence, and the last few days on the run had made him realize that he had the will to push through his fear.

Clumsy at first, he brought his left arm back and struck the monster with all his might. His metal fist collided with the Hollow Man's teeth, the sound grated the air around them.

The Hollow snapped in annoyance, lunging forward with its maw open wide. Giant teeth closed around Lukos' left arm, and his heart faltered, bracing for the pain. He turned his eyes away and saw the girl, frightened, watching him with awe. There were worse things to die for.

Lukos heard the clash of metals and felt his arm go numb. Several members of the Fox Den gasped. He looked back at the Hollow, which seemed confused. Four of its giant teeth were bent where it had attempted to tear off his arm, which was still attached with teeth marks cut into the metal skin. He and the Hollow stared at one another, realizing the tables had now been balanced.

"Fight back!" Kit cried. "Do it now, Lukos! It won't stop forever!"

A snarl emitted from the monster, but Lukos had already made the first move. He aimed a jab at those teeth, and then another at its blank face, leaving dents where his fist had been. The Hollow reared, fanning out all four arms and swiped at Lukos, picking him up off the ground. Lukos grabbed one of its arms, squeezing the metal as hard as he could. The Hollow wavered as Lukos rent its forearm in two. A black mist seeped from the broken arm.

Seeing the Hollow was again shocked, Lukos continued his assault, taking the arm he had ripped away and driving it into the beast's segmented torso. The first and second time it hit were like attacking a brick wall, but the third time the torn metal found a niche in the armor, and Lukos' preternatural strength drove the forearm deep inside.

The Hollow Man groaned, blackness evaporating from the wound in its torso. It held tightly to Lukos, refusing to let him go without a fight. Once again it brought him in, his head dangerously close to its mouth. Lukos pushed himself away as the two struggled, gaining and losing strongholds.

All it would take was a few inches forward and Lukos would find himself in pieces.

He took a chance. Reaching inside its mouth, Lukos

ripped at its teeth. It couldn't bite him if there was nothing to bite with. With huge gaps in its ghastly smile, the Hollow grew frustrated, tossing Lukos to the side. He landed against a wall, crumpling to the ground. The beast tried to leap away on its powerful hind legs, but slipped, with an inky blackness rolling out across the factory floor. Its arms clawed to pull itself forward, failing as they slowed to a stop.

Kit rushed to Lukos, with Pan not too far behind.

"I'm okay," he lied as the two looked him over. Kit checked his head and his arm, fussing all the while, ". . . stupidly running to get yourself killed . . ." as Pan studied his arm, seeing the metal skin for the first time.

"What are you?" he asked. Kit and Lukos froze, watching him carefully until he broke into a grin. "You . . . *You* killed a Hollow!"

Lukos looked over at the body. It had stopped moving, still leaking mist like a body draining itself of blood. "I almost didn't."

Pan laughed, falling back on his haunches. "Well that's because you fight horribly. But that can change."

"No," said Kit, threatening. "I know what you're thinking. He's not a weapon, Pan."

"Kit, you realize what this means? He can kill them! This changes everything." Pan's eyes searched Lukos. "What do you say? I'll teach you how to fight, how to survive. Help me save them!" He gestured at the Fox Den, some of who were gathered around the dead Hollow, while others checked their trade goods.

Lukos thought back to the saloon, the patrons' screams echoing through his head as he remembered the roof collapsing under the Hollows pursuit. A more recent image ripped to the front of his mind—Biggy's small body, being lifted from the ground by the metal leg jutting from his stomach. Lukos glared at the dead Hollow.

His voice came low. "I'll do it."

Pan and Kit both studied him; Pan with excited fascination, Kit with fear. Lukos didn't like either look.

Jimmerson approached their party, eyeing Lukos' metal hand. "We should keep moving. They'll only send more after this."

Pan clapped the man on the back. "You're right. Let's

get to the rendezvous and hope Mr. Tom was as lucky as the rest of us."

"Another failure," O'Toole muttered, slamming the cover closed over the sheath in front of him.

Shopmeister Hamilton Shorn coughed nervously, his legs twitching. "A failure, perhaps, Shekelton, but also a partial success. The project seems to be missing a few key ingredients, if only we could put our finger on it. My alchemists are growing closer, baby steps—"

"I'm tired of baby steps, Hamilton. The kings are close to raising their Mr. Lucy now that Lukos is of age. We must be prepared."

"Prepared for what?" asked a voice from the door. Both nobles looked up to see Miss Ash standing in the black doorway. O'Toole wondered how long she had been there. He glared at Shorn.

"Have you not learned to close the damn door when entering this room?"

The little man trembled. "My apologies, I thought I had."

"No matter. Get out and get back to work."

Nervously, Shorn nodded and sped past Miss Ash as if she were a snake waiting to devour him.

O'Toole neither welcomed nor dismissed the brothel owner. "I assume you have a reason for being here."

"I do. May I enter?"

He waved at the open door. "I cannot stop you."

"Thank you." She smiled sweetly, although it had no effect on the man. "I am curious about your preparations, my lord."

"The reason you are here, Ash. Out with it. And close the door."

She pulled it to with an audible click. "Don't be so insensitive. You and I might not have so many differences."

"I doubt that."

"Hear me out." She threw the morning's news down on his desk. Two pictures showed ruins of the Rusted Rose and the auto factory, headline screaming in bold letters, FIRES SWEEP ACROSS INDUSTRIAL, TWENTY

BELIEVED DEAD; MORE INJURED. "Five of those were my girls. The only reason they died is because of Zeb's appetite for destruction. I know you've thought about what happens when Mr. Lucy arrives."

"You're telling me you wish Mr. Lucy not to be woken up?"

"I want to restore the world as much as you do. But some sacrifices are unnecessary. I heard about Doyle."

"Yes. I have put the restraints on Mr. Zeb from this point forward. He has lost much of the freedom he was accustomed to as my attendant."

"Don't underestimate him. He is more powerful than you realize, even in his current state."

O'Toole sat down, seeming at once to be exhausted. "What would you have me do, Ash? Trust *you* of all people to help me?"

"I cannot ask for your trust. I am aware of that. But you and your alchemists cannot achieve the goals you seek by yourselves. I can help."

"And in return?"

"Nothing much. My desire is not for power, like some

of the others. I just want to see the world live again."

O'Toole narrowed his eyes. He could not trust any of the attendants, it was simply not natural. But he had been using their services for decades now. Working them against each other was dangerous, most certainly foolish. Still, he was running out of options.

"I will consider it," he told her.

Unsurprised, Ash nodded. "Thank you." She turned to leave, pushing the door open wide. Pangs of fear immediately flooded the room, setting both Ash and O'Toole on edge as the hinges creaked.

"Good morning, Ash," said Mr. Zeb. His face was shrouded in the dark shadows cast by the giant clock tower gears, eyes shining orange from the glow of a musky cigar.

"Zeb. Good morning to you as well. Did you enjoy yourself last night?"

"Oh yes. Perhaps I should have come to your pleasure house sooner, my dear. It's a pity about the girls."

Fires flickered in Ash's eyes, and not from the light of his cigar.

"Ah, yes," said Mr. Zeb, putting a hand to his hat brim,

"I came to tell you, my lord, that LaCrucis found their camp this morning."

O'Toole stiffened. "And?"

"Sadly, he has not recovered Lukos yet. He found the boy, but did not see Tom Vix anywhere nearby. It's a delicate matter—nab one and the other might run away. Knowing LaCrucis, he will want to do it with one sweep of his hand. Grab the boy, destroy the traitor."

"I will not indulge your game of cat and mouse, Zeb. Tom Vix, while a thorn in our side, is hardly as important. His chance to appear center stage passed years ago."

"LaCrucis knows what he is doing, I swear."

"And what of the children?" asked Ash.

"Children?"

"Tom Vix has created a safe haven for street children that would not have survived in Limbo by themselves. What will happen to them?"

"Don't play the fool, Ash. LaCrucis will cleanse the aqueducts of their sewage."

Ash's nostrils flared. She looked long and hard at O'Toole, who dipped his head only slightly.

Chapter 7: Of Teeth and Promises

"That matter aside," said Mr. Zeb, "what were you both discussing? Anything of interest?"

"No," said O'Toole. "Nothing of any importance."

Chapter 8: Rest for the Weary

It was colder here, the Lake of Fire now hidden from them by several cavern walls. And while most fugitives would have taken comfort by passing into darker tunnels, away from the water processing system's frightening light, they were being hunted by things with no reliance on things such as the convenience of sight. As such, they derived no comfort passing into the next cavern chamber.

The Fox Den moved through the darkness, blending against the rocks and rusted structures. This camouflaged movement had become their second nature, nearly as easy as breathing for them. Scouts ran ahead, young children with soft steps and keen ears that could make themselves invisible as they went. Every few yards, the rest of the Den would hear the tiny clicks and whistles and move forward knowing the path was safe.

Kit kept an eye out for Mr. Tom or the frog-like Hollows—Big Teeth, as they were called in the underground—as they traveled. She also paid close attention to Lukos, gritting her teeth as his boots trudged against the uneven ground. She could feel the other Foxes growing weary of his noisy presence in the midst of their silent march. He was like bait to a trap that didn't exist, and she was the useless tripwire.

Up ahead, the scouts had not given the signal for some time. Though they made no sound, Kit could feel them become restless. She reached for Lukos . . .

Whistle, click, click.

She sighed, carrying on.

Kit stole a sidelong glance at Lukos. Killing the Hollow earlier had shown her what she needed to see—Lukos had the will to live. *Strong, handsome. Kind. If only he didn't move like a clunky rubbish bin.* The man's senses were dull, and yet . . .

Again, no sound came from the scouts at the front. Snapping out of her stupor, Kit listened, waiting . . . nothing. Unwilling to take uncalculated chances, she retreated to the tunnel wall, pushing Lukos into a nook. A few others did the same, the effect spreading until the only thing sitting in the tunnel were the two remaining carts. Steam hissed gently from the valves while gears turned in a muted chorus. They had been reworked for more stealth than the average machine up top.

A shape stumbled into sight, barely visible. It shuffled forward, whistling once.

"It's Mr. Tom!"

The Foxes peeked out from behind their rocks and shadows slowly, a couple at a time.

Pan's lanky silhouette appeared. "You're alive!"

Mr. Tom's voice sounded like worn cloth brushing against the tunnel walls. "Should think so. Slipped down a crack below one of the aqueducts. Thought I was a dead man, but it probably saved my life. Sewage masked my smell."

"I'm sure! I can smell you from here."

"Oh, is that right? Perhaps you can sniff us out a place to rest with that big nose of yours."

"What about LaCrucis?" Kit called, creeping from her hiding place.

Mr. Tom squinted in the dark, tapping his walking stick in thought. "He's out there."

The tunnel grew quiet, considering this. The angry howl of a faraway Hollow reached them, setting everyone on edge. Together, the Foxes started their movement again, a creeping swarm around Pan and Mr. Tom.

"You really do stink," Kit muttered, now a few feet away. Lukos held his breath so he couldn't smell anything.

"You realize how bad this is," Mr. Tom said.

Pan chuckled. "Lukos must be some sort of celebrity to cause this much trouble." He turned a look toward Lukos. "Or did you steal from the wrong person?"

"He isn't a thief," pressed Kit. "He's hardly a criminal of any kind."

"Ha! Likely story with all of this fuss."

"It's true," Lukos said with a nod. "All I did was leave my master's house without permission."

"Who the hell was your master?"

"Sir Patterwicke Doyle," Lukos and Kit both intoned.

"Keeper of Industries," completed Lukos.

"The Keeper of Industries!" Pan whistled low. "A noble! Well brick me over the head and call me Patty."

"I'd rather not," whispered Lukos.

Ahead of them, Mr. Tom growled. "Would you all shut up? I'm trying to think." They recoiled into a sulky silence, and he continued. "This isn't a simple chase. This isn't a couple of pickpockets getting away from some authority. They will never stop hunting you. Either of you, damn it. You can't stay with the Fox Den, Kit. You know that."

She nodded, her eyes resigned, but frightened. "I know."

"Wait. You can't mean through the hole?" said Pan, his voice raising a little.

Mr. Tom sighed. "It's precisely what I mean, boy. Use that thick skull of yours. LaCrucis is in the mix."

"What's the hole?" interjected Lukos, feeling ignorant.

Another whistle, this one high and shrill. The Foxes scattered—Kit, Pan, and Mr. Tom expertly dropping their conversation and blending against the walls. Lukos pressed himself into the side of the tunnel, trying to imitate them. He held back a pained grunt.

Two humanoid figures crossed in front of the tunnel, far ahead of them. It was followed by what was without a doubt a Hollow — the type the Foxes called Big Teeth. He only wondered who the two figures were, until he caught sight of the glowing red eyes. Then came more Hollows, but another type that Lukos couldn't see very well, a type he didn't recognize.

The tension was palpable, but the three Hollows were oblivious to the Foxes, too far ahead to notice any of the refugees. They passed quickly, leaving Lukos with more questions than security, and a new level of paranoia. He saw Kit share a glance with Pan — the two nodded, continuing on silently — and wondered why he felt that pang again.

Lukos shook his head. All that mattered was moving forward and not getting caught. "So. What is the hole?"

"It's how we trade with the smugglers," explained Mr. Tom. "It's the hole in the wall of Limbo. The hole that leads to the outside world."

"What outside world? There isn't anything outside of the wall." Lukos laughed.

Kit sighed. "Lukos, after everything else you've learned, would it really surprise you that there is life outside of Limbo? That whole lie about being the last group of surviving people after the Great Destruction . . . Well, it's just that. A lie."

"You can't be serious," Pan said, looking between Kit and Mr. Tom. "You can't let her go. She won't survive out there."

"She'll never have a chance in Limbo, Pan." Mr. Tom's voice sounded sad, strained. "We'll talk more of it later. For now, shut up and let me think."

Leaving the tunnel was like crawling out of a dumbwaiter after a week. The air was no more fresh than it was inside—and if anything it smelled of natural gas, a mildly unpleasant stench that Lukos could not place at first. The gas smell clicked when the Foxes turned off the mechanical carts and started hauling them on manpower. No one wanted to go up in an accidental blast.

However, it felt better to get out. The narrow passage had felt like a one-way death trap, begging for the Hollows to find them and pin them in. Here, at least, he felt that they had better chances of escape.

It also meant they had to keep sharper eyes and ears in all directions.

Mr. Tom sent out some of the faster children, scouting for a place to stop and rest.

"How much farther?" Lukos whispered to Kit.

"Not sure, they haven't come back yet."

"No, I meant to the hole."

"Oh." She paled, becoming grave. "A long ways."

Pan chuckled. "Not used to walking this much?"

"After a day spent running for your life?" Lukos snapped. "No."

"You'll get used to it."

A series of clicks hailed them from ahead. Mr. Tom answered with a short whistle, and Chloe appeared, big eyes shining proudly.

"Found a spot!" she said, excited.

He ruffled her tangled hair with a calloused hand. "Good job, girl. Show us the way."

George sat at his desk made of newspapers and a giant rubbish container. Business was slow after the events of the previous day. Many were still grieving those who died in the fires, and the rest were avoiding the streets for fear of the heightened Hollow activity. George himself knew that he shouldn't be conducting business at the moment, but he stayed open for those in need. He kept some jackets, gloves, other bits of clothing, and a couple of rough sacks filled with loaves of bread behind his makeshift desk. The boy wondered how Kit was doing.

A rough looking man with bad teeth ambled into his alleyway, hands stuffed into the pockets of his worn coat. "'Ello, Georgie."

George narrowed his eyes. "Don't call me that."

Allwurst guffawed. "Sorry, sorry, forgot you were all grown up now. How's business been, kiddo?"

"Stop bricking around. What do you want?"

"What?" the man asked, his face falling. "No old times? No catch up for old Allwurst?"

"I run a shop for merchandise, not a saloon for gossip. Now what do you—"

"Well, that's just it actually, Georgie ol' pal. Gossip. I need to know something."

George narrowed his eyes. Allwurst had never been a Fox he fully trusted. The man was treacherous. Useful, skilled in his roguishness, but a lying sack of shit if George had ever known one. And he knew many. "That's not the trade I deal in. You'll have better luck at some bar or somethin'."

"No, see, I know you're still connected." Allwurst slunk closer, looking over his shoulder. "I need to know where the Fox Den is, Georgie."

"It's George. And I don't know where they are."

Allwurst laughed nervously. "Well no one *knows* where it is. But you could tell me where they've been. I'll pick up the scent from there."

"I have no clue where they've been, and even if I did know, why would I tell you? You know the rules. Once you're out, you're out."

"I want back in."

"Why?"

"Look around!" Allwurst took his hands out of his coat

and spread his arms wide. George quickly glanced at his hands. He relaxed. No weapons. "You heard all the madness that happened, didn't you? The factory over on Blum Street exploded last night, Hollow Men crawling around it like ants. My cousin worked in that hellhole, and I still haven't heard from her. The Rusted Rose is gone, too."

"I know, yes, times are violent and harsh. It's Industrial. It'll settle back down to mildly life threatening in a day or two. You'll be fine."

"Georgie—I'm sorry, George. Please. I'll pay you if I have to, I don't feel safe." Allwurst dug into his coat, throwing a gold card onto the rubbish bin's lid. George reached out for it, but stopped, pulling his hand back. Allwurst smirked a little, then threw a second gold card out, and a third on top of that.

"See, this is why I can't tell you," said George with a smile. Allwurst had shown his hand. "No one with three gold cards on their person needs to get into the Fox Den. What are you playing at?"

The smirk slid right off Allwurst's face. "Listen here you little shit—"

"No, you listen. I don't know where the Den is, and I don't know where it was, but something strange is going on in this town and I won't have anything to do with it. If I were you, I'd steer clear of it too, whatever your gamble is. Judging by your coin, I'd say someone wants you to find them, and I shudder to think who wants to use you, of all people, to find the Den. So go brick off."

Allwurst whipped forward, one hand grabbing George by the collar, another holding a pocketknife to his neck, chipped but razor-sharp, already drawing a red trickle mixing with the dirt caking his neck line. "Smart as always, you little bugger. I suppose you're proud of being so clever. But here's something you might not have deduced with that squishy muscle between your ears: You can tell me without me cutting you, or you can tell me after I've started cutting off pieces-parts."

George swallowed, the knife digging a little deeper.

"So what'll it be, kiddo?"

"Beneath the factory!" said Georgie. "The one that burned down. That's where they stopped last. Headed for the Lake of Fire."

"If you're lying—"

"I'm not! Why do you think that factory burned down in the first place? You're looking for Kit, right? That's where she went to join them! I swear!" George gasped, feeling the knife slide against his skin, and clamped his eyes shut.

Allwurst's eyes bored into the boy, searching for deception. After a moment, he threw him backward, knocking over the seat made of newspaper bundles.

George gulped down air, holding a hand to his bleeding neck.

Allwurst waved his knife in the air, other hand swiping up the three gold cards. "Like I said, if you're lying . . ." He drew the flat edge of his blade against his own throat.

The small businessman said nothing, watching the crook with angry, frightened eyes.

As Allwurst left, George prayed that his misdirection would buy Kit and the Den a little more time. He started bundling up his merchandise. It was no longer safe to vend here.

They dined on fruits and vegetables stolen from the markets above. Lukos bit into a pale apple with a decided lack of passion, wishing he could have the same gusto as David, who savored every slice of his red orange with a smile. So far since running away, Lukos' experience with food had been either a near-death experience or simply edible. He wished he had nabbed a few different spice bottles from Doyle's kitchen on the way out.

To his right, sitting cross-legged on the cavern floor, Kit ignored another orange.

"What's wrong?" he asked, and she snapped out of her trancelike gaze.

"Nothing."

"Hardly looks like nothing."

"We're being chased by people and things that seem to want you alive and me dead, and they are so relentless that they aren't afraid to destroy life and property while doing it."

"Meanwhile," said Pan, joining them out of the blue,

"your boss man tells you the only way to survive is to leave everything you know behind and go outside the wall!"

"So . . . nothing," said Kit. "Nothing is wrong."

"That's a whole lot of nothing," Pan whispered to Lukos.

Lukos leaned back on his palms, balancing the apple on his thigh. "I'm excited to leave Limbo, now that I know there's a world still out there. I was so ready to leave Doyle's service and experience the city, but it's rotten and horrible."

"So is the rest of the world." Mr. Tom, who had appeared behind them with a weary look, sat down between Lukos and Pan. Neither he nor Kit would look at each other. "You're naïve, Lukos. That will get you killed, and it will get her killed. Hell below, if we can't get rid of you fast enough, it might even get the rest of us killed."

Lukos' ears burned as he fiddled with his apple. "I won't let that happen."

Mr. Tom laughed, long and bitter. "It's not a matter of letting. You want to take your fate, our fate, the world's fate into that metal hand of yours? Good luck. What you need to realize is that whatever pretty fantasy is in that brain of yours just isn't going to come true. Even the best don't make it out without losing bits of themselves. So stop dreaming kid, and start fighting."

"Because that saves everyone," muttered Kit.

"Nothing saves everyone." Mr. Tom's tone turned harsh, full of ire. "But it's better than simply hoping it will all turn out okay, and it's better than running away from the people that need you."

"Is it? Tell me, when was the last time you actually fought for your cause? All you do now is thieve and hide!"

Lukos looked between the two as they silently shot fire and lightning between each other, catching Pan's bemused look in the process.

Finally, Mr. Tom's expression returned to his weary, sad slump. "We'll leave in a couple of hours. Get as much rest as you can." It wasn't clear whether he was speaking to all of them or just Kit, but he was already on his way, a group of children crowding him at one point to give him hugs and *goodnights*.

Kit watched on, an expression staining her face that

Lukos couldn't read. She huffed, standing and stalking away with a graceful spin on her heels.

"Are they always like that?" asked Lukos.

Pan chuckled. "Fiery souls, those two. They've always clashed, but she was always Mr. Tom's favorite."

"They don't hate each other," Lukos observed, "but they act like they try to. I don't understand."

"Yeah, well, you haven't lived through everything we have. You can't understand. Suffice it to say that Mr. Tom is right. Life bricks you over, and all you can do is try and move forward with the people you love." Pan looked over at Kit, still marching. "It gets harder when they don't want to stick around."

Even Pan started to look dejected, sad. Lukos felt his heart beat a little quicker, seeing how he watched after Kit. He could see desire in those eyes, and resignation.

"What happened between them? Why did she leave the Fox Den?"

Pan sighed. "You might as well know, since the two of you are traveling together. But don't you dare tell her I said anything."

Lukos raised his hands defensively, nodding once.

"There was a girl named Emily. She and Kit were like sisters, and Mr. Tom sort of raised them both. I'm sure you know how Kit is. Master thief and all that jazz."

"She stole my pocket watch off me. That's how we met."

Pan grimaced. "How sweet. Anyway, Emily was not a master thief. She was a kind soul, not good at much of anything. Mr. Tom liked to keep her down here when the other kids would go and pickpocket. But Kit snuck her out sometimes, trying to teach her something. Trying to help her friend find a skill, you follow?"

Lukos followed all too well. On the run with Kit these past few days . . . he felt useless most of the time.

"As you would expect, one day Emily got caught. She and Kit were in the Business District, picking the pockets of wealthier men, trying to make a real score. But one of them caught Emily by the hand. Right old bricker, he was. He held her there and grabbed the attention of a Hollow Man. Kit was a young girl then. She just stood there as two Hollows escorted Emily away into the shadows. Kit followed them all the way to the Oudemonium. What exactly happened to Emily was never found out, but you and I both know how Hollows are."

"That's horrible."

"Kit blamed herself, of course. It didn't help that Mr. Tom blamed her too. Said she disobeyed him, that she should have left well enough alone. And then she told him she was going to leave. He told her, in turn, that if she left she would regret it."

"Did she?"

"Did she regret it or did she leave? I can't tell you if she regretted it, but I can tell you she was gone the next morning. I couldn't believe it. Was afraid that one day I'd hear news that she'd been caught. Never thought she would actually come back."

It explained a lot. "So that's why she keeps to herself. She's afraid of other people dying around her?"

"Wouldn't you be? I wouldn't go reading into it too much, though. She's a complicated girl, Kit."

Lukos looked over to where she had bedded down for the night. "Yeah. She really is."

"Well, it has been one hell of a day," said the young revolutionary, standing and yawning abruptly. "Something tells me tomorrow isn't going to be any easier. Night."

Lukos was left alone with a half-eaten apple and some rocks. "Yeah, goodnight."

Chapter 9: Up in Flames

O'Toole strode through his bioalchemists' laboratory. The rooms alternated between dark and light, hot and cold, hosting admixtures and containers sensitive to their environments. One started to bubble as he walked by, popping loudly and releasing a hiss of air.

Lords Shorn and Carlisle huddled with one of the head bioalchemists, their frames tense from focus. Shorn, his tiny legs jittering, looked as if he might himself pop from excitement. Even from the opposite side of the room—this one a brightly lit, cold room with metal tables and green walls—O'Toole could hear the small noble's excited murmuring.

"How goes the journey?" asked O'Toole, startling the three men.

The bioalchemist smiled. "My lord! I had no idea you were coming today. We're testing another serum now."

O'Toole grunted, approaching to stand by them.

A large rat struggled in one of the man's hands, the other hand holding a large syringe. With fast, steady movements the alchemist jammed the needle into the rat, emptying it. It squealed and bit at the metal, but the pain was over as quickly as it had begun, and the rat was lowered into a small labyrinth.

"Did it work?" asked Carlisle.

Shorn hushed him, stern. "Nobody knows yet, you ninny! Be quiet and watch."

O'Toole's eyes narrowed, seeing that the rat was coming onto the first trap. To its credit, the creature sniffed at the trigger—a tiny trip wire, and turned down a different avenue in the maze, only to step on a pressure plate. The walls of the labyrinth shot forward with spikes, skewering the rat the length of its body.

"Wait for it," whispered the bioalchemist. He flipped some switch near the labyrinth and the spikes retracted, leaving the dying rat to collapse onto the metal floor. But as they watched, its sides, covered in growing patches of red, started to ripple. Previously dead, it squeaked, nose twitching, and stood—its stab-wounds already having healed—and carried on within the labyrinth.

Carlisle gave a suave chuckle, but O'Toole told him to be quiet. The rat took a few more turns, steering clear of the traps. The men watched with stressed anticipation. After several more seconds, the rat's sides began to bleed again, its wounds reopening.

"No!" hissed Shorn.

The holes in the rat widened, with the creature losing its ability to walk as the skin deteriorated well beyond its original injuries. It began to shed its fur, skin bubbling, exposing the bone. The rat began to dissolve before their eyes.

O'Toole nodded to himself, and left without another word, leaving the three men to stare and watch as what little of the rat was left melted away.

"Right, so, you need to learn how to fight."

Lukos watched as Pan spun the bamboo stick in his hand.

"I'm assuming I don't get that," he said, pointing at the stick.

"You aren't as dumb as you look, you know that? Now, when you fight another human being, it's all about taking away their ability to fight and increasing your opportunity for flight." Pan swiped the stick in front of Lukos' face, inciting an intense flinch. "See? You just closed your eyes for a second. I could have kept on, had my way with you. But Hollow Men, those are different. They don't flinch."

Lukos rubbed the back of his neck, embarrassed. "So how do you fight them?"

"Mostly, you don't. You run. Opportunity for flight, remember?" Pan circled Lukos, who followed with a cautious gaze. "Or you distract them while your friends are running, and then you escape after. For all their speed and strength, Hollows do tend to be a little narrow-minded. I think it's their armor. Gives them tunnel vision, as far as I can tell."

"But you've killed them, obviously."

"Yes. It can be done. But we try not to."

Lukos frowned. "Why?"

"Hollow Men are cruel by nature, and when they find us, we're easy targets. We don't always carry around loads of explosives, Lukos. You have no idea how lucky we were to have those this time. Weapons like those are hard to come by."

"Then what am I supposed to do?"

"Hush, I'm still trying to figure that out."

Pan stopped his circular pacing, tapping the side of his jaw with the bamboo, deep in thought. "You see, what I do . . . I just don't get caught. But I'm faster and better than you are at this sort of thing."

"Sure," Lukos said, sour.

"Here's the thing, old buddy, old chap. You have something that the Hollow Men don't."

Lukos looked down at his arm. "This?"

"No, their entire body is metal, Lukos. No, you have fleshy bits, and you have a life to lose."

"And how exactly is that supposed to help?"

"It isn't! Or maybe it can. Either way, the point is, it takes a lot to take a Hollow Man down. But you, you're easy to kill. Feeling any better yet?"

"Pan . . . no. No, I'm not."

"Good! Now maybe you have a little more perspective. So here's what you're going to have to do. You have to hit more. Hit faster. Hit harder. Overwhelm them from the start. That's your best chance."

"We are talking about the same monsters, right? They're usually the overwhelming ones."

"Yeah. Just means you have to step up your game. All right, lecture over. Knock me down, any way that you can."

Lukos put his fists up. "Okay. How?"

"Oh, brick, did you not hear any of that? Come on!" Pan rolled his eyes and swung with his bamboo stick, a surprised Lukos barely jumping out of the way. A few more swings were joined by a combination of punches. Lukos couldn't dodge them all. He took a mean jab to the jaw, feeling the bamboo slap his neck before he tumbled and rolled several feet back to avoid Pan altogether.

"Stop running away! Fight! I won't stop. The Hollows

won't stop!"

Pan kept coming, growling, swinging his arms wildly, with more ferocity than his previously displayed grace. Feeling a nervous itch in his shoulders, Lukos ducked and rammed into Pan's torso.

"Not good enough!"

Crack! came the bamboo across Lukos' back.

Suddenly, Lukos felt the heat flush into his face. He hooked a left into Pan's gut, then a right. *Crack!* Again came the bamboo. Lukos reared up, grabbing the bamboo with his metal hand and ripping it from Pan's grasp. Then he grabbed Pan by the shirt and tossed him several feet. Surprised, the young thief lost any landing he might have had, tumbling to his side, going limp.

"Pan!" cried Lukos, rushing forward.

Pan rolled over, giggling to himself. "Now that's more like it. Okay, let's go again."

Seeing the bits of people and Hollow Men scattered

around the old waterworks building didn't surprise All-wurst — he'd seen his fair share of carnage living with the Fox Den before. But this last Hollow — the one with its own arm buried in its chest . . .

Well, this is new. What could do such a thing? Certainly none of the Den members. Another Hollow Man? Do Hollows even fight each other? He didn't care to find out.

Allwurst looked up from the dead creature, his face scrunched up in deep thought. Their trail from here had gone cold again.

He played with the gold card in his pocket. The feeling of power it gave him was intoxicating. After this job, he would be set for life. Maybe he would even try to venture outside Limbo. Get out of the murderous den of criminals that was Industrial.

He shook his head, pulling his thoughts back to the route. If he knew Tom Vix, the old fox had to know that the nobles were involved with this new, young runaway in his beloved Fox Den. Which meant Vix would be taking every cautionary measure he could.

Which, in turn, meant that he was taking an emergency

route. *That* route.

A loud clang from inside the waterworks set Allwurst's teeth to grinding. Mammon had promised that the Hollows would not bother with him. That he had a sort of *"temporary immunity"* as that pale, spectacled freak had put it. Still, a lifetime of fearing the Hollow Men was not forgotten easily. At least it wasn't LaCrucis breathing down his neck. Allwurst knew that monster was down here, somewhere in the cavern. He only hoped he never had to see the thing.

Allwurst planned out the movements in his mind, shortcuts through the machinery and tunnels. "Sorry, old man. Here I come."

His face was wet, suddenly and without warning. Lukos didn't have time to register that he was waking from the deepest, most peaceful sleep he'd had in weeks, or that he was gasping for air, or that his eyes burned from the droplets. He only knew that his face had just been doused with frigid water.

Standing in front of him, with her bucket still dripping, stood the culprit, laughing. "Wow," Kit managed between laughs, "you don't jar awake pretty, do you?"

He wiped a layer of water from his eyes and cheeks — eyebrows sticking up from the affair — and slowed his breathing, trying to calm his panicked heart rate.

"I'm sorry." Her amusement told Lukos she wasn't. "Some people were taking advantage of the downtime to clean up. You seemed like you needed the sleep, though, so we just let you be."

"So you splashed me in the face?" he finally asked, voice gravelly. His shoulders ached from sparring with Pan. "Ow, ow, ow!"

"It wasn't personal, I just figured you would want to wash your face while you could. I don't know when we will be able to next. Pan beat you up?"

"Yeah, a little bit."

"Even more reason to wash you off, then."

Lukos sighed, the cold seeping down past his shoulders now. "Thanks. I guess. Although a little warning would be better next . . . wait, something's different."

He studied her, realizing it was her hair. Lukos had a distinct image of Kit in mind—pale, big brown eyes, black ruffled hair. But now her hair was red, and smooth. At first he wondered how she had managed to change the color, and why, before he understood that she had simply washed it clean. After several seconds of silence, she narrowed her eyes, seeming to get defensive. "Are you just going to stare, or do you have something to say?"

"Sorry! It's just . . . I didn't know you had red hair. It's . . . it's pretty."

Kit's expression, usually so sharp and ready to strike, softened, a different hue appearing on her cheeks. She laughed it off. "Mr. Tom wants to move again as quickly as possible. If there's anything you need to do before we leave, hurry about it."

Less than half an hour later, they departed, Lukos having just finished washing the rest of himself down in a nearby drip of water. He grabbed another apple for breakfast, his stomach complaining. Meat—anything with meat—sounded fantastic right then.

The Fox Den grew even more cautious than usual,

Lukos noticed. When he asked Kit about it, she nodded, glaring at each formation of rock, every shadow. "There are certain routes we never take. They are scouted, recorded, and planned, but only used in emergency."

"This is one of those routes," Lukos said, following.

"When you live underground, running in giant circles all your life, it can get repetitive. Even when there is constant danger, there's a comfort in knowing what comes next. But then you take a path that's new . . ."

"You leave your comfort zone."

"Right now, no one is in their comfort zone."

"Speak for yourself," whispered Pan from behind them. His eyes were just as wide, glancing up at the ceiling every once in a while. "I'm always comfortable with my surroundings."

Kit spared a moment to roll her eyes before returning to the shadows. He tried to slide between her and Lukos, but Lukos refused to move over. Surprised, and a little grumpy, Pan crossed to stand at Kit's other side, instead. Lukos refrained from glancing to the side.

Soon after, the rush of water could be heard, and the

temperature began to rise steadily. A layer of fog began to dance at their feet, growing thicker. Lukos found himself perspiring, his arms growing heavy. At the front of the Fox Den, Mr. Tom looked over his shoulder. "It's close."

The water grew louder as they approached, until Lukos could hardly hear himself think, and then even he looked over his shoulder, no longer being able to hear if anything was closing in on them. Light poured from around a curve ahead of them, flickering over the stalagmite silhouettes, the accompanying fog playing tricks on the eyes.

He watched as the Fox Den switched to communicating through hand signals. Some of the adults behind Mr. Tom made straight lines with their hands and the children obeyed, filing into a line of pairs. Pan tugged on Lukos' sleeve, pulling him to the back of the line with some of the elders, while Kit moved ahead. In his mind, Lukos could almost hear them say it—*protect the kids.*

The line began to turn the bend, disappearing person by person; the light growing brighter, the heat stinging more with every step. And then it was his turn. Before him was a large river housed within tunnel walls, roaring with not only the rush of water, but tongues of flame. A hot mist expanded from the river, splashing onto the rocky ground and walls, rising to become the thick, sapping fog.

Feeling lightheaded, Lukos reached out to lean against a wall for a moment, but recoiled. The stone was uncomfortably warm to the touch, the hot moisture clinging to his palm quickly evaporating.

Pan clapped Lukos on the back, laughing at the shock. Lukos could not hear his laughter at all.

Up ahead, Mr. Tom was already at work, his cane lying on the ground, although it took Lukos a while to understand what he was fiddling with. Some of the adults, including Kit, had joined Daniels in pulling a system of well hidden chains and crude levers. It looked like hard work, sweat dripping from their brows as they strained to push and pull at whatever device or devices he could not see. Lukos took a step forward, intending to help — after all, he might as well put his left arm to use if he could — but Pan held him back.

Lukos cocked his head in question. *Why not?*

Pan pointed two fingers, first toward his eyes, then

toward the bend in the tunnel that they had come from. *Keep watch.*

Remembering that they were being pursued, Lukos turned, dutifully watching their tail. He shook his arms and flexed his metal hand, preparing for the worst and hoping he wouldn't have to live it. He glanced behind, watching in amazement as Mr. Tom, Kit, and the others worked to lower a small metal bridge — just big enough to fit the steam carts — from the darkness of the ceiling, suspended by thick chains and cables. Air tanks floated the bottom, presumably to keep it afloat during passage.

He could see why this was an emergency route. The idea of crossing a flaming river, rushing along with such ferocity as to be completely deafening and probably injurious to fall into, if not lethal, over a thin, suspended metal bridge . . .

They're all insane, thought Lukos. He grinned, nervous butterflies in his stomach. *It's brilliant.*

Pan clapped him on the back again, and Lukos refocused. He trained his sights on the bend. The Fox Den was counting on him.

Then somebody crashed into him. Startled, Lukos looked to see the Fox Den scrambling. Children clung to the adults, who had already begun to retreat from the river. It wasn't long before he saw why.

LaCrucis.

At an inhuman pace from the far side of the river, his left leg pumping out great trails of steam and dirty smoke, LaCrucis ran for the bridge. His gleaming eyes were bright and white, unblinking, staring, and steady even in his jostling speed. Mr. Tom was waving his arms frantically, Den members raising their weapons. The sudden *BOOM* of the first shot, loud enough to overtake the river, seemed to cause Lukos' blood to flow in his veins again. The following gunfire kept his heart beating.

LaCrucis paused, holding his own mechanical monstrosity of an arm up to shield his face from the gunfire. With his other arm he raised his gunsword, firing into the Fox Den, his pace slowing to a brisk march. One of the women firing her rifle jerked backward, blood splattering over the rocks as his shot found purchase in her neck.

Mr. Tom grabbed a large blade from a nearby steam

cart, grim-faced as he raised it high. He brought it back down on top of the chains they had used as pulleys. It bounced off, Mr. Tom looked around at his followers, screaming something — silent against the river, but red with passion. He hacked at the chain again and again, others grabbing their own clubs and hammers and swords to join him.

Kit pushed Star and David back toward the tunnel entrance, huddling other children in front of her, ready to take a bullet in the back if that was what was asked of her. Pan was doing more or less the same, trying to make his way toward Mr. Tom and the others while getting the children to retreat. LaCrucis fired again and a large man holding a club fell, his body slipping into the fiery river.

Taking a deep breath, Lukos rushed to help.

LaCrucis took his first step onto the bridge, taking aim at one of the few who remained firing at him. The man's side plumed blood and he dropped his rifle, which Pan picked up and kept firing. Lukos felt his heart trying to crawl through his throat. So much death and pain, and it was *his* fault. His mind conjured images of Kit or even

Pan falling to their death with gunshot wounds, each one worse than the first, shredding his nerves. When finally he reached the Fox Den, their eyes wild and dripping with sweat, Lukos pushed them aside and grabbed the chains with his left hand. A bullet whizzed by his pants leg and Lukos lost his nerve for a moment, raising his gaze. LaCrucis was looking directly at him, aiming to injure.

The boogeyman stopped for a second, cocking his head in question. Lukos did not have time to wonder why.

Ignoring mortal peril, he squeezed and pulled at the chains, trying to destroy them with a single bare hand. The others saw what he was trying to do and rushed forward to pull the metal links to the ground, pinning down the section they had been hacking at. Lukos understood, seeing a length of chain that was in poor condition. He began to punch it with all his might, crumbling the rock beneath the section. Another shot buried itself into the rock by his feet, but he kept going, finally seeing one link give way, snapping. The broken chain flew up into the air, whipping hard against the rock. The bridge shook.

LaCrucis began to run again until shots pelted him.

A blackish-red blood seeped from wounds in his torso. Lukos began to hammer at the ground faster, desperation starting to sink in. It would be for naught, he knew, if LaCrucis was allowed to cross the river.

The monstrous figure crouched and, with a great mushroom of steam from his mechanized leg, launched into the air, closing a great distance of the bridge. Lukos smashed another section of links, and then another, the bridge swinging away from the crossing now, tilting wildly. LaCrucis was shaken to his knees, nearly being thrown into the river. He stood, steadying himself, hateful blazing whites set intently on Lukos.

With a final blow, Lukos smashed the final length of chain, the broken end of which flew up into the ceiling. The bridge shifted greatly, caught for a moment as the now-unseen chains knotted in the above ceiling, then wrestled free. The suspended metal crossway became a floating deathtrap above a fiery rapid. It shook and crashed against rock walls, quickly disappearing from sight beyond the river's bend. The Fox Den watched LaCrucis, as the monster communicated rage and hatred through his silent, concealed glare.

Lukos stumbled back against a wall, not caring for the moment how the rock burned hot through the shirt on his back. Mr. Tom, Kit, and Pan took a few seconds to catch their breath, looking to him with varying degrees of suspicion and gratitude before they were on the move again, guiding the Fox Den back the way they came.

Taking a final look over his shoulder at the flaming river, Lukos wondered what their next step would be and how any of them could survive much more.

Chapter 10: Like Lambs

What are we supposed to do now?"

"If they knew about this route, who's to say they don't know about the other emergency routes!"

"Of course they know. They're toying with us."

"My wife is dead."

"It's because Kit came back with that freak!"

"We're bricked!"

"Why did she have to die?"

"It's over, isn't it? This is it?"

"The Hollows will be here any minute."

"LaCrucis will destroy us all."

The Fox Den rang with clamorous voices, afraid, angered, lost. Lukos grabbed Kit's hand, ready to flee if the Den became a mob. As for the Den's leader, he stood motionless, looking over his flock. Silent. His eyes, usually hardened and sure, were lost in thought.

"I know of a way!"

The Den's panicked din quieted as Pan stepped into the middle.

"There's still time. And honestly, at this point, it's as good a chance as any. I mean, we all know it—the Hollow Men have us pinned. So we catch them off guard. We cut right through the middle."

"Isn't that where the Hollow Men come from?" asked David, the small boy having to shout through the crowd to be heard. Beside him, Star shivered and rubbed her arms, looking cold and dismal.

One of the adults, a man with a shaggy blonde beard, answered. "No. That's where the staircase is, and the lift. We could all be seen."

Lukos leaned into Kit, whispering, "The staircase?"

"It's a dangerous place," she said.

"We've already been seen!" Pan continued. "And if we just sit here, or if we try some other route, we'll be seen again, and they'll be ready for us this time. If we cut through the staircase, then maybe—"

"No!" Mr. Tom shouted.

Pan fell silent, looking at his mentor with a readied stubbornness.

"Boy, you don't fully grasp what we're up against."

"I know what we're up against. It finally happened. LaCrucis—the big, bad wolf, is at our doorstep, just like you always warned us about. So we have to move, we have to move fast, and we have to do it hard."

"Taking that path . . . there are worse things than Hollow Men, Pan. There are worse things that LaCrucis. He's just a mad dog compared to the others."

"Then what better idea do you have?"

"We try another route."

"We don't have time!" Pan's brow knitted with frustration. "Kit was right. You don't have the fight in you anymore. You just hide."

Mr. Tom fell quiet again, his mouth slack.

Pan turned to the Fox Den, slowly looking over the crowd. "We go through the staircase." He pointed at Lukos. "We fight with what we can. We run. We survive."

"And what if we die?" demanded the bearded man.

"Then we die."

The Den watched Pan with varying shades of fear, admiration, and frustration.

"Whether we like it or not, we're caught in a game unlike any other in Limbo. I certainly wouldn't have chosen to play, and I know none of you would have either. Fact is, we're here. Now, I don't know why he's important," Pan said, gesturing at Lukos. He chuckled. "As far as I can tell, he isn't. Guy has a shiny arm, so what? But the nobles seem to think otherwise. We've been forced into a corner, and they've killed our friends. But we'll continue on, in spite of them. Might as well give them a little hell while we're at it."

As the Den hung on Pan's every word, Mr. Tom's shoulders slumped more and more. This was the boy that he'd raised to fight back, the man that would succeed him in leading the Fox Den. This is exactly what he had raised Pan to become.

Kit led Lukos away from the rest of the group as the Fox Den came to a consensus.

"Why does it sound like we're walking into a death trap?" he asked her.

"Because you are," said Mr. Tom. Lukos and Kit both jumped, having not noticed the old war hero join them. "There are beings that serve the nobles. LaCrucis is the most vicious of them, but his mind knows only rage and hate. The others are crueler in the way they plan."

"I think I know who you are talking about," said Lukos. "I grew up under the watchful eye of a woman named Bell Begor. She came after me when I ran away from Doyle. I saw her body pierced with glass, and her neck and spine snap in an explosion, only for her to get up and keep looking for me."

"Good. Then you've already seen things many men would not be able to believe. Begor is one of the more dangerous of the nobles' attendants. She is like LaCrucis — she moves in straight lines toward her goal, leaving wreckage in her wake."

"How many are there?" asked Kit. "Why didn't you ever tell us about them?"

Mr. Tom looked at Kit, eyes full of sadness. "There

are six. I worked with them in the war, Kit. They've been my enemies since then, but after years living underground disturbed only by the occasional Hollow, I never thought they would personally bother with the Den."

"And then I came along," said Lukos.

"Boy, you have to understand that people will blame you for many things, myself included, but it is not your fault. You cannot blame yourself, either, or you will stumble and die when your feet hit rough terrain."

Kit squeezed Lukos' hand. She had been one of those people, after all.

"This staircase," Mr. Tom sighed. "They've built a lift through the center of it, and they traverse it often, taking down kidnapped street dwellers, bringing up riches, weapons, and monstrosities. It goes up to Limbo. It also goes down. Deeper down than the Lake of Fire."

Lukos frowned. "Down to what?"

"Down to the end of the world, Lukos. When we cross it, you will see. The fates willing, we won't be caught by any of those monsters on their way up or down in that damned lift."

Allwurst couldn't believe it. Never in a hundred years would he have thought the Fox Den would willingly cross the staircase.

Now he faced a predicament. Continue following them into one of the most dangerous places he'd ever known to exist, or let LaCrucis and the Hollows take over and chance losing Mammon's reward. If Mammon was to be believed, of course, then the stairs would pose no threat to Allwurst.

He made up his mind.

"One last job, right?" he asked himself. "You're practically done."

He took from his pocket the small winged lizard, feeding it scraps of meat, mindful of his fingers. As its tiny brass jaws finished gobbling up the food, Allwurst wrote a quick note, rolling it into a small scroll.

"Take this to Mammon," he whispered.

The lizard screeched in a voice that was part gurgle, part grinding clock parts.

It was no simple homunculi inside that small, ornate shell. The lab-grown creature had been trained well, and knew the layout of the entire city, and beyond. It sped through the air, leaving behind hot smoke trails that dissipated fast, finding the nearest aqueduct. Within minutes, it sailed into the late, domed sky of Limbo, taking a bird's eye view of the city. Zeroing in on a location, it coiled into a dive, hurtling to the earth where its master would be waiting.

Mr. Zeb slunk through the back door, making sure to keep the grime from his boots local to the doormat. He took in the drifting aroma of pie and warm tea with milk and honey, still savoring his last snack. A servant passing by the washroom caught sight of Zeb and picked up her pace, fingers gripping the basket she carried a little tighter.

He smiled. While his old manor had only partially been burned to the ground, O'Toole was staying true to his word and keeping Mr. Zeb on a short leash. He was given a small apartment on the western wing of O'Toole's own residence. It was lacking in privacy, but Mr. Zeb didn't mind. Since becoming a "guest" here, the fear and grisly rumors that had always swirled around Mr. Zeb only grew, becoming nastier, more depraved. He hoped the increasing discomfort of O'Toole's servants would get back to the archduke soon.

The afternoon sun shone through the windows, revealing a swirling flow of dust and lint as Zeb marched through the mansion, up the grand staircases, and through rich halls. It was not that O'Toole's servants were lazy or inattentive — in fact, they worked hard to keep the place clean. But the place was almost unlived in. An empty thing impressively decorated, shared with no one. The archduke himself was hardly ever around, locked away in his Oudemonium most of the day and night.

It was true that Mr. Zeb was a new resident to the mansion, one that set O'Toole's servants on edge, like a Hollow Man in a room full of convicted criminals. However, he was quite familiar with the place.

Mr. Zeb climbed the marble stairs that led to O'Toole's

private chambers. It was colder here, the temperature dropping with each step, and the floors were dusty. Not dirty—no, there wasn't enough foot traffic for it to ever get dirty. After all, the only two allowed to come up here were Mr. Zeb and O'Toole. The landing for this part of the house was dark, the oil lamp sconces full, having rarely seen the light of their own flames. Double doors, imposing, full of authority and culture, stood between the unlit lamps. They creaked, mournful, as Mr. Zeb made his way into the master suite. It was dank inside. And, unlike every other neatly-sectioned fragment of O'Toole's life, it was a deplorable mess.

Snuffed-out candles led into the room in some strange pattern that was neither circular nor straight, chalk lines sketched between a few of them, threatening to climb one far wall. Some were still intact—charms and sigils of protection similar to the ones in the Oudemonium—but most had been partially erased.

Lavish sheets hung between the tall, mahogany bed frame and the floor, ending in a twisted pile on top of a rich, Asian rug, which itself was covered in stacks of weathered papers and old books left open to specific pages. Upon an old wardrobe and cabinet set, an untouched glass sat next to a bottle of scotch, which had not been so neglected and was now empty, its crystal stopper lying in between the two. Drawers were left half open, socks and other garments spilling out of them onto the floor. Mr. Zeb's eyes scanned O'Toole's private bedroom carefully, clucking to himself. The man had been stressed beyond the usual.

He got to work, starting with the candles and their wax, which he scraped from their pillars and the spillover onto the floor with a practiced ease, then scrubbed the chalk lines clean. During a trip downstairs, servants gave him nasty, terrified looks as he passed them by with sponges, soapy rags, and other cleaning supplies.

As O'Toole's personal attendant, his private quarters were Mr. Zeb's to care for, and Mr. Zeb's alone, a duty he carried out a few times each week. The other servants were not allowed here, and for a multitude of reasons. O'Toole did not want anyone to see his weaker moments, those unorganized stacks, empty bottles of various drink, an unkempt abode for a well-kept man. That, and . . .

Mr. Zeb's eyes glanced over the cause for the room's nippy temperature. A large metal box—more like a metal closet—extended across an entire wall, locked tight and radiating with frigid air. O'Toole's entire reason for existence, encased inside this bunker, inside this disheveled room. The thought amused him.

The stacks of papers and books, Mr. Zeb carefully bookmarked and set aside on a nearby bookshelf. The titles and texts spoke of alchemy, the black arts, and enlightenment. Several were gifts from Mr. Zeb's own collection, bestowed upon O'Toole in the archduke's search for power and control.

It was no quick task, taking care of the other rooms within the suite where O'Toole's slip into madness had blossomed into apparentness. But he did not mind it. Despite toying with each and every one of the nobles in some way or another, Mr. Zeb had a soft spot for O'Toole, remembering the young revolutionary and his mad ambitions to change Limbo, and his twisted notions of saving the world. He was an interesting man.

Mr. Zeb finished with the bed, changing its sheets, fluffing and tidying the pillows, and making it presentable again. He left the master suite worthy of an archduke, closing the doors gingerly on his way out. A prickle in his gut told him that company was not far away.

Downstairs, he found Mammon waiting impatient in the main foyer, the butler uneasy in his demeanor at speaking with him, while eyeing the strange winged automaton on his shoulder. Mammon's crystal stare bored into Mr. Zeb.

"Where have you been all day? I've been trying to find you."

Mr. Zeb spread his arms wide. "And find me you did. What is it, Mammon?"

Mammon's fingers twitched at his sides. The butler excused himself, neither needed nor wanting to remain among the nobles' attendants. "There has been a development."

Mr. Zeb's eyebrow arched. "And? Spit it out, man."

"Vix and his little raiding party are crossing through the middle." He paused. "We'll be able to intersect them ourselves."

"Ah. Good job, Mammon! A favor, paid for in gold?"

"It was an investment. What is mine will be returned to me in time."

"As always. As for the Den, Let LaCrucis handle it."

The automaton's ticking heartbeat became more pronounced in the silence. Even with Mammon's eyes completely behind those green spectacles, Mr. Zeb could see the irritated confusion. "But, we have them within our grasp."

"And within our grasp they will remain, old friend. Trust me. They aren't getting away, no matter how far they manage to run. Would you care to join me for dinner?"

Pan leaned over the cropping of rock that Lukos had found to nap under.

"It's time."

Lukos sighed and nodded, rolling out from underneath his hiding spot. "Why do I feel like this is a horrible idea? I don't even live down here and I feel like we shouldn't be taking this risk."

"Well, you're right. You don't live down here. So have a little faith. This is our best option. And be on your guard. You're our protector now. Until we turn you loose at the hole, anyway."

"No pressure."

"None at all." Pan spun on his heel, a mask of collected calm hiding the jittery spirit of a young man who believed he could change the world. Lukos looked for fear too, but either it was lacking, or Pan hid it well. The Fox Den was brimming with nervousness as it was. It would only get worse if their fearless leader reflected their worry.

Lukos's knees buckled, something having crashed into the back of them. He spun quickly, already back on his feet, metal hand clenching, bracing for a fight. Another ambush . . .

. . . only to find Kit laughing at him. "It's me, relax. Or don't. You're our sword and shield now, apparently."

Lukos breathed slowly, heart racing to equal his own fear. "Kit, I don't know if I can do this. Just because I killed one Hollow doesn't mean I can defend the entire

Fox Den."

"Of course you can't." She grabbed his hand, pulling him to where the community of thieves had started their latest departure. "And Pan is silly to give you that impression. But we've all learned something about you."

"What's that?"

"That you can fight back."

His hand slipped from hers. "What happens when we cross the wall? Neither of us know what's out there."

"I've heard stories."

"Stories aren't the same as actually being there, Kit. I've lived under Doyle's thumb for two decades. The idea of Limbo in my head is very different from what I'd always dreamed of."

"And yet, you survived. We'll learn, we'll adapt, and we'll live. It's what I've always done. I'm pretty tops at it, if I do say so myself."

Lukos had come to the conclusion that Kit was tops at pretty much everything. "I'm just worried, is all."

"We'll manage."

They fell in line behind one of the steam carts. Up

ahead Lukos could see Chloe, Star, and David clinging to Mr. Tom. The Den seemed grim, their usual stealth replaced by the simple sense of unspoken fears.

"This is a bad idea," Kit whispered.

They passed through the caves and tunnels unheeded for hours, passing rock and machine alike. They had to change direction once, circling a giant pit that fell deep into the earth, large tubes pouring filth into it. Lukos marveled at its immense size and the depth of its void, glad he was not alone. Mr. Tom never took the lead, the image of a tired man waiting for whatever fate had in mind.

At the front of the Den, Pan marched on, resolute. Lukos tried to feel his confidence, telling himself that everything would be okay. LaCrucis' hate-filled gaze flashed through his mind, assuring him that it would not be.

In the distance was a large wall of sorts. Unlike the last rock wall, it radiated not heat, but cold, and Lukos could see that it curved back at the edges. He couldn't see how high it went, extending well beyond any of the dim light that the Den carried with them. It looked like a huge cylinder. They headed toward a hole in the wall.

"Is this it?" he asked Kit, quiet.

She nodded.

Closer and closer they drew, until Lukos could see that it was not a simple hole in the wall. It was an archway, and no poor craftsmanship had carved it into the rock. It was wide enough to let several men pass through side by side, and taller still. One of the giant Desidious Hollow Men could fit through, he knew, with little effort or stooping. The sides of the arch had been carved to look like thick columns, running up into a triangular pediment. The columns were covered in creatures that Lukos knew from Doyle's library: Snakes, ravens, centipedes, rats, as well as a few others he could not place. On the pediment, crafted to look as if they were resting there, were gargoyles, some insect-like, others reptilian and avian. They laughed or screamed in their static stone poses — gnarled, hairy legs gripping the ridges of their perch.

Lukos shuddered. "What is this place?"

Kit didn't answer. Maybe, he thought, she didn't have one to give.

Chapter 10: Like Lambs

The archway swallowed the Fox Den, scarcely lighting the inside of its void with their torches, revealing walls that had been carved into masses of grotesques, similar to the ones on the perch, only bigger, and somehow worse for the imagining. The stone monsters were all crawling over each other, pushing deeper into the tunnel. The Den followed their hellish path.

Chapter 11: The Devil's Ladder

When the Rusted Rose burned to the ground, some of Ash's girls lost their lives. Many lost their place of work. Some, however, stayed properly employed, for theirs was not the industry of flesh, but of information.

Like Jasmine.

Jasmine had always been intelligent, swift and . . . *skillful.* In one of the hundreds of bamboo gardens that produced Limbo's clean air, Ash listened to the olive-skinned girl relay everything she had learned about Lukos and Kit. They sipped on a light, pink hibiscus wine, a regular gift to the garden's owners from the Arts District's alchemic botanists. The spot itself was ideal, a nearby trickling pond providing their conversation a muting sense of privacy.

"Do you think Kit will be all right?" Jasmine asked,

having finished.

Ash thought for a moment. "I don't know. I hope so. The girl has always been stubbornly resilient. Thank you, Jasmine, you did well."

The girl smiled, taking the stack of gold cards from Ash. "Anything for you, miss. What's my next assignment?"

"I need you to find the house of a man named Allwurst. He hangs around Industrial bars."

"I know the one. Leave it to me."

"Thank you. And Jasmine?"

"Ma'am?"

"Be safe."

The former brothel girl nodded, disappearing into the street masses.

Ash peered up at the glass dome sky, streaks of moisture just visible. It was going to rain soon.

Leaving the pleasant atmosphere of the bamboo garden, she hurried along, making her way from the Arts District to the center. Once more, the Oudemonium stood before her. She grimaced at the thought of the metal symphony inside, still missing sorely the piano duels and the cabarets of the Rusted Rose.

A few minutes later, she stepped out of the lift. O'Toole's door was shut.

The man grows more paranoid with every passing breath.

Before Ash's hand fell upon the strange metal to knock, the door clicked open, and O'Toole began to step through. His eyes widened when he saw Ash, hand immediately at his breast pocket. Fast as a serpent, she grasped his arm.

"Relax. I'm here to talk, not harm."

He struggled under her grip, but Ash was stronger by far. Finally, he stopped, the malice in his eyes softening. "I'm sorry. The last days have been taxing."

"I'm sure. Finding out that your Fountain of Youth makes lab rats explode and melt probably is not very reassuring."

The malice returned, dripping through his stately features. "How do you know about that?" he growled.

"Shekelton, you know me. Are you really that surprised? You should also know I can help solve the problems your bioalchemists can't wrap their simple minds around, before Zeb and the others find out."

He snarled. "Blackmail, then, is it?"

"Close your mouth." Ash was starting to get impatient, her eyes flashing—quite literally—with fire. "I am not some simple whore that gets by with information, Shekelton, nor am I here to antagonize you."

Chin raised, O'Toole waited as she simmered down.

"I do ask for a favor," she finally said, softer this time. "When LaCrucis catches up with the Fox Den, you leave Tom Vix and Kit to me."

Mammon was upset.

He understood Mr. Zeb's reasoning, but he was tired of waiting. They had waited for so long.

Sitting on the staircase, time flowed differently. He watched below, discerning the landing, waiting for the Fox Den to emerge. He would not interfere. He would only observe.

The gusts of air surprised Lukos. They pushed and pulled at his clothes, causing the tarps atop the steam carts to rustle louder than anyone cared for. The Den was already on edge. No one needed more reasons to be afraid of the dark.

In the rocks above them, to the sides—even below their trodding feet—the imps, snakes, insects, and birds continued along with them, some looking up, their faces carved to grin at any passersby. Lukos couldn't tell if the grotesques in the walls were encouraging the group forward, or warning them to turn back.

"I don't like this place," Star whispered. "It feels bad."

Mr. Tom patted her shoulder gently, keeping a steady watch both in front of his flock and behind. He grasped his cane tightly, fingerless gloves revealing protruding white knuckles even in the lowlight.

A light appeared at the end of the tunnel. Not bright by any definition, but distinct. The gusts grew more steady, chillier.

Pan gestured for his front line of men to keep walking, falling back to the steam cart and grabbing several explosives. Kit tried to catch his eye, but he was either too focused or purposefully avoiding her. Returning to his place in the Den, he distributed the bamboo explosives, sharing a serious glance with each of them as he did. Others took out their weapons, brandishing blades and clubs, making sure their guns were loaded and ready. Lukos could feel the anticipation.

Following a signal from someone on the front line, anyone with a lantern put it away. The tunnel went dark, but there was not much ground left to cover. What ascended and descended beyond that dim archway became more visible, to the wonder and horror of everyone who looked upon it. As the Den passed from the claustrophobia of the tunnel completely, the staircase came into full view.

It was not like anything Lukos had expected. Neither could he explain the intense desire building deep inside him to scream at the stairs at the top of his lungs. He gripped his own metal hand, struggling to breathe, eyes following its horrid spiral.

It was massive, wider even than O'Toole's Oudemonium above ground. The staircase descended and ascended, deeper and taller than their eyes could follow; white as bone, every visible surface etched with unnatural writings. It spoke of antiquity, and a strength that found time and wear irrelevant. Lukos' was no architect, but he could tell that it was much older than anyone in that chamber could imagine, well before the Civil War, or even the Great Destruction. A metal and glass shaft, obviously built in times more recent, hung in its center—the lift that Mr. Tom spoke of. Each step was about Lukos' height. Whatever built this staircase, whatever walked its damned spiral, was not . . .

He struggled to complete the thought, reluctant to, his breath hitching.

This was not meant for human beings.

"Stop staring," hissed Kit. "Don't think about it. It'll brick your mind faster than anything you would imagine. We have more important things to do right now. Like leave."

Lukos shook his head, mentally apologizing. He wasn't sure if it was for Kit or for himself. "I don't understand."

"No one does, but we're not going to get into it. We're

going to leave this wretched place behind, Lukos." Her voice was sad, almost desperate. The sound set his feet in motion.

The other Foxes filed in, avoiding the impossible vision before them as best they could. It was obvious that many of the children had never seen it before. Tears dripped over their small cheeks, mouths agape until the adults wrangled them forward, whispering to keep moving.

In front of them stood a strange kind of natural landing connected to the stairs. It stretched across the cylindrical chamber like an uneven spider's web, several pathways of rock stretching to make suspended pathways, leading from six other tunnels spread in a circle, tunnels much like the one they had just come through. Between each path of rock were great gaps that reached down into an abyss. A great stairwell, Lukos surmised, though how far down it went, or where it led, he dared not ask. One misstep, one trip in the wrong direction, and he would plummet to the undesirable answer.

They walked along one of these narrow pathways, drawing closer to the center of the room — closer to that bone-white horror, making Lukos' skin crawl.

He moved as fast as the momentum of the group would let him, which seemed hurried already. They were all eager to leave this place.

Allwurst had rushed to get ahead of the Fox Den. He crouched, nestled into one of the pediments between two carved imps, trying desperately to ignore the whispers that had begun to invade his mind.

He nearly whimpered when he saw them appear. Tentative, they stepped from the blackness of one of the seven tunnels. Allwurst fumbled in his jacket for Mammon's intricate long pistol. He was to leave the boy alive. That might be a challenge. The rest were free reign.

The Fox Den started across one of the narrow suspended paths, and Allwurst began his climb down. *Where are the damn Hollow Men when you need them?* he complained to himself.

He took aim, looking down the long barrel toward the

head of the group. *Who better to aim for than that snot-nosed brat?*

Mammon sensed the incoming wave of hatred in the air, joined by others of like kind; felt the fire in his bones. His anticipation was palpable. It had been years since he had seen LaCrucis at work.

Perhaps, just perhaps, this would all end now.

"There!" cried Daniels. "You, stop!"

He raised his gun as the others looked to see who he had yelled at. Coming from one of the other narrow paths was a ragged looking man with a pistol.

"Stop there, Allwurst, I don't want to—"

Daniels never got to finish his sentence. A hole appeared in his head, which rocked backward as he fell to the ground, dead, his rifle clattering over the edge and into the abyss.

The Den's reaction was immediate. Children screamed, running to hide behind the steam carts as Foxes brought their weapons to aim. Then, someone cried out those dreaded words . . .

"Hollow Men!"

Allwurst was no longer the problem. Lukos looked around and saw teams of Hollows streaming from three of the darkened arches that gave entrance into the stairs' chamber. The big-toothed, froglike Hollows, but also another humanoid group. Hollows that looked similar to LaCrucis, but thinner, and missing the coats and hats.

Lukos shook his head in despair, seeing how fast they moved to the center of the chamber. *There's no way we'll make it in—*

"Hurry!" shouted Pan above the growing clamor. "To the center! Run for the center!"

"He's going to get us all killed!" shouted Lukos, but Kit tugged him forward, running.

"No! He's right, if we can clear the middle before they do, we can fight defensively, bottleneck them."

"Kit, look how many there are."

She ignored him. Her face, like every other member of the Den, was grim and determined. There was no turning back. He understood. There would be no easy escape here.

The main concern was for the safety of the children. The adults ran at a steady, measured pace, taking shots against the Hollow Men and Allwurst, who seemed to be working in tandem, though the traitor seemed overly nervous. Their gunfire did little more than make Allwurst tremble and hide.

Lukos looked again. They weren't far from the center. *Maybe this isn't impossible. Maybe we can still make a clean get away.*

"Almost there!" cried Pan, leading his people fervently. He looked back through the crowd, eyes wide with adren- aline, finding Lukos.

Lukos understood. He pumped his legs harder to get through the crowd, boots feeling heavier every second. Kit kept up, her leg starting to hurt again. Even with the Den's constant medical attention, the fall from a factory window was still a recent occurrence.

And then they were at the center.

The stone connected with the stairs unevenly in several places. They chose the path that slanted downward, facing off against only one of the oncoming groups of Hollows — the so-called Big Teeth. The steam carts picked up speed, rolling faster with the subtle decline.

"Whatever you do," Pan said, raising his voice over the clamor, "don't touch the stairs! Stay on the rock."

They wound around the staircase, following its crooked landing and forgoing several of the small paths that shot off from its center. Lukos wondered which of the chamber's seven archways they aimed for, growing increasingly worried about the nearing Hollow Men.

This is as far as I go. I did what you want, Mammon, your bloody monsters can take care of the rest.

Allwurst shook with fear as he moved against the swarm of humanoid Hollow Men. He had never seen this type before — their movements were smooth, not jerky like the other Hollows, and their eyes blazed white. Unlike the skeletal Callidus Hollow Men that primarily patrolled Limbo, these had faces that were mostly featureless, and the ornate shells of their bodies seemed an attempt at human anatomy. Each carried a thin saber at its hip.

These were no ordinary Hollow Men, if ever there was such a thing.

He spun around, watching the Fox Den try to make their escape. They circled the staircase now, just over halfway through the chamber. Allwurst felt a pang of regret—he knew most of those men and women, and the children. The Hollows would show them no mercy. He hadn't quite thought about how this would end before now.

It doesn't matter. I'm a rich man, now. I can finally leave this hell.

Allwurst shook his head, pulling away from the Den, and turned to leave.

A single figure blocked his path, approaching fast, every step a focused, deliberate action. At first, Allwurst thought it another one of the strange Hollow Men—he had the same blazing white eyes—but he quickly saw that he was wrong. This one wore a long coat and a wide-brimmed hat, his right arm and left leg larger mechanical pieces. He carried a pistol with a long bayonet attached.

A new wave of terror struck Allwurst to his core. "LaCrucis," he whispered, voice hoarse. He moved to the side to let the boogeyman pass by, but LaCrucis raised his weapon, looking directly at Allwurst.

"W-w-wait, I'm on your side! I'm with Mammon!"

The gun exploded with a puff of smoke, and Allwurst felt a punch in his chest. He cried out in pain, raising his pistol. "Bastard," he gurgled. Before he could fire, LaCrucis swung his blade, and Allwurst's arm — still clutching the firearm — fell hard to the ground.

Allwurst stumbled back, but was caught by the cannon-claw that was LaCrucis' right hand. The thief tried to ask, "*Why?*" but as the metal talons dug deeper into his chest, he found himself unable.

LaCrucis brought the man close. Through the metallic smell of his own blood, Allwurst inhaled death and decay. The monstrosity growled long and deep, white eyes searching Allwurst's face for something.

And then, LaCrucis tossed the thief like a broken doll.

His vision fading, the last thing Allwurst saw was the staircase as he plummeted into the depths of the earth.

"This is all assuming LaCrucis hasn't killed them yet." O'Toole stared at Ash over the top of steepled fingers.

"He hasn't. Mammon and Zeb would know about it."

"You realize what you are asking. My personal feelings aside, you will still have to deal with the nobles if you intend on keeping Tom Vix alive for more than anything but questioning."

"I'll worry about that when the time comes. Right now I only need your word that Vix and Kit are mine."

"I could care less for the girl," O'Toole sighed. "Fine. If —*if*, Ash—if he comes back alive and in one piece, then you can have Tom Vix. I don't know why you still care for the traitor, especially after all this time."

Ash shrugged. "Love is a strange thing, Shekelton. Even for me." She stood, crossing to the door.

"Hmph. Love and lust are two different things, Ash.

When will you start working with my alchemists?"

"As soon as I see that they are both safe."

"Then let us both hope for sake of time that things down below are progressing smoothly."

Chapter 12: The Slaughter

LaCrucis strode through the crowd of Hollow Men. They were too distracted, focusing only on moving forward. He grabbed them with hand and claw alike, shoving them over the side. One of the Edactus Hollow Men — the froglike Hollows — snapped at his hand. It realized its mistake too late, right before LaCrucis aimed his claw at its face, releasing his chained cannonball into its metal skull. The ball embedded, he yanked his arm to the side and flung the Edactus over the edge.

The surrounding Hollows parted to give him a pathway. His Saevus Hollow Men followed him, falling into military file, marching forward.

The staircase loomed above them, a sentinel waiting to observe the massacre below. Lukos couldn't help but see it in the corner of his eye, even while focusing on the end goal.

At the back of the Fox Den, a well-aimed explosive kept the first Hollow at bay. They fought with their backs to the archways now, facing the center of the chamber and moving in reverse. As they had hoped, the Hollow Men had bottlenecked behind them, a river of gnashing metal teeth, flailing arms, and marching legs swarming around and over the staircase's rocky landing. Those that touched the stairs seemed to change the way they moved, if only slightly — maybe faster, smoother, or maybe moving slower than molasses. It was impossible to tell.

Some of the Hollows had broken off to the other suspended walkways, aiming to cut the Den off before they reached one of the archways.

"Lukos, deal with them!" Pan waved an arm through the air frantically. "We'll hold the back!"

Lukos nodded, pushing his way to the other side of the Fox Den. He recognized these new Hollows. He had seen a concept sketch floating around Begor's office—a simply designed Hollow, nothing flashy like the others, but with a highly detailed body. It was the most human looking Hollow Man he'd ever seen, with the metal shell segmented to imitate muscles bending, flexing, and moving. It had been labeled something. He struggled to remember, facing down his possible doom.

Saevus Hollow Man.

Looking at the real thing, he could see that the designs were successful. Their movements were too human, and for that matter, too focused, unlike the other monsters Lukos had seen. Two of them rounded bends in the pathways, coming for him fast.

I can't do this, I can't do this . . . How am I supposed to fight these? I'm not strong like Mr. Tom, or fast like Kit, or creative like Pan.

"Lukos!"

He looked behind him. Star had pulled an old metal bar from one of the carts, a tool to help remove the wheels for repair, and tossed it to Lukos. The mix of fear and belief in the young girl's eyes pierced his heart. That's what he would fight for. Her eyes widened.

"Look out!"

Lukos spun, readying himself. The two Hollows were there, pulling sabers from their sides. The first engaged, blade raised above its head. Lukos held the iron bar up to block, taking a step back. The saber cut through the iron like paper, and Lukos was glad he'd taken a step back.

He lunged, ramming what was left of the bar into the Hollow Man. It clanged against its skin, jarring him and sliding to the side. Not even a scratch.

The Hollow reared back, pointing the blade at Lukos' center of mass and thrust forward. Lukos held a hand out thinking he could catch the blade, and he did, pulling it to the side so that it stabbed only the air beside him, but not without searing pain.

Both Lukos and the Hollow looked down, surprised. The Hollow was surprised at Lukos' strength and daring. Lukos was surprised himself, shocked at the blood that dripped from his metal fingers. While it had been scratched, dented, and otherwise beat up, his left arm had never been cut before.

The Saevus Hollow retracted the sword and Lukos cried out as the serrated edge dug deeper into the meat of his palm. The machine slashed through the air as Lukos ducked beneath its legs, nearly finding himself skewered on the blade of the second Hollow. He leaned left as it slashed right, hacking into the first Hollow's leg. The creature let out an angered scream—one that sent a shiver down Lukos' spine. Unlike the other, more bestial sounds that he'd heard from Hollow Men, this one sounded almost *human.*

But he didn't have the time to dwell on it. Seeing that the sabers could damage their wielders, Lukos was mentally mounting a new strategy.

Both Hollows had turned toward him now, and he was caught in the middle. One hesitant move, he knew, would be the end. Before either made a move, he attacked the one with the wounded leg, punching and leaving a dent in the detailed abdomen, then turned to see the other attacking again. There was no time to move.

The first blow came from above. Lukos blocked with his left arm, a thoughtless reflex, sloping his arm at the last moment. The blade glanced off his forearm, but not before slicing off a peel of metal skin. He gasped in pain, but the Saevus Hollow was already attacking again, swinging from the side this time. Lukos dove out of the way, and the sword buried itself into the other Hollow's head.

A ghastly screech that sounded neither human nor inhuman rang from the featureless monster. The inky mist that he'd seen before oozed from the Hollow, but this time it held a dark red hue.

Lukos looked at the red swathe missing from his metal arm, coming to a realization that both excited and disturbed him. *They won't kill me. They'll cut me all day long, but they cannot kill me.*

The second Saevus growled, now furious, kicking the other dying Hollow off its blade. Lukos rolled over to the body and grabbed the sword from its twitching grasp, raising it in time to deflect another downward arc. Both blades still dripped with his own blood.

His arms felt weak, and his legs were shaky as he scrambled to face off with the remaining Hollow, but he dared not lose, nor be distracted by the battle behind him. The

Fox Den was counting on him to clear the path.

The Hollow moved first, another wide swing. Lukos knew he was the weaker party here. He didn't try to block it, but daringly tackled the creature around the middle — it didn't budge. Lukos didn't care. He was inside its guard, and he wasted no time in sliding his blade up into the thick metal chords that comprised the Saevus Hollow Man's neck. It gurgled as it fell back, ready to topple over the edge of the pathway. Lukos made a grab for its saber, and the two struggled on the ledge for a moment.

Someone grabbed Lukos around the middle, pulling him away from the edge, and together they wrenched the sword from the Saevus, letting the creature fall.

"That," panted Kit, "was possibly the worst swordsmanship I have ever seen in my entire life." She laughed, a sound wrought with tension. "Keep it up!"

He laughed, unable to find words, and handed her one of the blades. He glanced back to see the Den was using one of the carts as a blockade.

Both armed with weapons that could cut through the Hollow Men's shells, Lukos and Kit led the march forward. Behind the first two Hollow Men, a Big Teeth had followed, hopping great distances.

"Quick tip," said Kit. "Knock it over the edge if you can."

"How the blazes am I—"

He didn't have time to finish. A Big Teeth was there, its large jaws snapping greedily. Kit wasted no time, years of aggression and terror revealing itself in a few brutal slashes that removed four teeth from its oversized jaw. She kept going, the serrated blade slashing imperfectly, and the Hollow began to shy away. Lukos flanked it, hacking once, twice, three times at a single arm. It reared, standing and attempting an imposing stature, and—when Kit threw her shoulder into its middle—falling backward, grasping at the air.

"Like that," she said. She clutched at her leg, sounding pained. "Only it may not work the same way twice."

Lukos nodded. "We'll get creative then."

They were at a crossroads now, three separate streams of Hollows facing them down. If they could get the Den safely past this point, then maybe—

Star's scream broke all thought. Lukos' eyes searched the crowd. There, by the steam carts, the girl's hands were at her mouth and she was falling to her knees. Mr. Tom was there in an instant, pulling her away, though she fought him, kicking and screaming.

Lukos soon saw why. David.

The boy, who'd been helping to fend off the Hollows in the back, had been run through, a serrated saber cleaving through his side. A Big Teeth jumped forward, crushing the bodies of other fallen Foxes and began eating the child.

Flashbacks of Biggy's death streaked through his mind, and he tried not to see the others in the Fox Den who had died. While he and Kit had been fighting at the front, they'd lost so many.

"Lukos, look out!"

A metal fist connected with the side of his head, causing his sight to go black . . .

. . . for a split-second . . .

Enraged, Lukos pushed himself off the ground, finding the Hollow that had punched him. He jabbed his saber into its chest, pushing the body back, back, back, breaking through a small group of enemies with the momentum, using the Hollow as a shield. He grabbed the throat of the second with his metallic hand, crushing it with some difficulty. He released the one and pulled his sword from the other's chest, letting them both drop in front of a grinning frog. Lukos leapt onto the beast, thrusting the saber into its back as a lever to hold on to, and started digging away with his left hand, fingers prying at parts of the shell, ripping away small bits here and there. Kit's sword plunged through its eyeless skull, surprising him. Lukos could see the tears pouring from her eyes.

Mr. Tom handed Star off to Pan, swiping the explosive from the younger man's hands. "Go! Get them out of here." The archway was right there. They were nearly out of this hellish chamber. Pan dragged Star away, his face a tortured mask.

A single explosion detonated, driving the Hollows away, followed by another. Lukos joined Mr. Tom at the rear, jabbing at Hollows to keep them from progressing—a tangle of arms and swords and legs fighting for purchase against any human flesh they could reach. Taking a risk,

Lukos stepped forward, finding that their swords swung less. He was right. They were afraid of killing him.

"What are you doing, boy?" shouted Mr. Tom.

"Trust me! They won't kill me!"

A hand reached out, grabbing Lukos by the scruff of his shirt. Mr. Tom pulled him back, jabbing at the Hollows with his metal stick.

"Be that as it may, I think I'll stay close by, if you don't mind," growled the old revolutionary.

"I'm okay with that."

The two made slow progress. There was only one steam cart left—Lukos could imagine what had happened to the others—and Mr. Tom seemed set on keeping this one intact. Behind them, in the crowd of monsters, one began to emerge. LaCrucis, an embodiment of spite and chaos creating order around him as the various Hollow Men fell away to allow his passing.

Fear turned Lukos' arms loose, making him sloppy. Again, Mr. Tom pulled him back. "Now's the time to go," Mr. Tom urged. "He's closing in. This is our only chance to escape."

Darkness began to envelope them. They'd reached the tunnel. More unsettling carvings surrounded them as they passed underneath the rocky pediment. LaCrucis shoved Hollow Men out of his way, pulling his gun from its scabbard at his side and taking aim. An Edactus leapt forward, getting in his way. That Hollow met its fate as he ripped into it with his large claw.

"Get ready to run!" Mr. Tom shouted, loud enough for everyone to hear. He struck the bamboo stick of dynamite he'd been holding onto — it glowed with its lit fuse — and dropped it on the steam cart, then lodged the cart against the wall.

LaCrucis took aim once more.

With Lukos not far behind, Mr. Tom turned and ran as fast as his limping leg would allow, leaning heavily on his walking stick.

"*Brace yoursel—*"

The cart became a cluster of fire and deafening sound, hot air and smoke billowing, consuming everything.

Mammon descended the stairs from his high vantage point. The smoke was still clearing, with Hollow Men digging at the collapsed archway.

It's a shame. That tunnel was old as time itself. He was rather upset over it being so casually destroyed.

The long pistol lay on the ground, Allwurst's severed hand still grasping it. Mammon looked around, disappointed that LaCrucis had not entered the fray sooner. In fact, he hadn't seen where LaCrucis had disappeared to. If Mammon had to guess, he was probably already in another tunnel, chasing his prey.

He stooped, picking up the weapon and grimacing at the blood that had splashed over the beautiful engraving. *No matter. It'll clean easy enough.* He pried Allwurst's hand from the weapon, taking in a deep whiff of the arm's scent before wrapping it in a handkerchief and stuffing it in his pocket.

"Thank you, Allwurst. You did your job. At least, most of it. Now, show me where you left my gold."

Chapter 13: Forgiveness and Betrayal

It would have been better if they were fighting.

Mr. Tom only stared at Pan with a disappointed hurt, looking over what remained of his family. Most of the children had survived. As for the adults, only Jimmerson and Vasi had come out of that tunnel alive. The rest died to protect the next generation of thieves and scavengers.

But for what now? There was no Fox Den left. All of their steam carts had been left behind or destroyed. A group of children could not make it when they were practically on their own, not when LaCrucis had their scent.

Lukos hissed in pain as Kit finished wrapping his arm, pulling the bandage tight. She didn't know if it would matter—his arm had already stopped bleeding on its own. "This," she told him, "will at least keep dirt from getting in the wound."

Star ran up to Mr. Tom, clinging to him tightly, her partner in crime gone. The old man turned his agonized gaze over Lukos, who had to look away, and then Kit. She held his gaze, unmoving, tears in her eyes.

"What do we do now?" asked Vasi. "Everyone is dead. Our livelihood is gone."

"We have to get back to the surface," said Jimmerson. "Start new lives up top. There's no life left for us here."

"Everyone shut up," snapped Mr. Tom. "We're going to the hole. Daniels. David—everyone who just died by the hands of a Hollow. Their death will not be a waste."

"But how? There's no point in going to the hole anymore. We don't even have anything to trade with the smugglers!"

"I have a plan." Mr. Tom scanned Pan, Kit, and Lukos again. "Enough rest for now. A group of Hollows that size won't stop until they've found us again."

He limped away without another word.

Kit looked at Lukos, scared.

"I'm sure he'll think of something," Lukos reassured

her.

"That's what concerns me."

Lukos stood, pulling her up with him. They had both kept their sabers, Lukos tucking his into his belt, Kit tying her cape in such a way as to create a makeshift harness on her back. Together, they approached Pan.

"I'm so sorry," he whispered at their approach. "This . . ." Unable to finish his sentence, his shoulders shook with grief.

Kit crouched, gripping his shoulder, and the three of them waited there like that, letting the remnants of the Den pass them by.

"Everyone followed you of their own accord, Pan. They knew the risk just as well as you did. Now get up, move on."

"I'm sorry," he continued. "I think I understand now. How you felt when Emily died."

"Pan, don't. This is not the time."

He nodded, wrapping his arms around her.

Lukos left them to their moment, feeling their sadness ripple over him in waves. They would catch up when they were ready.

"You called, my lord?" Mr. Zeb stood in the doorway. The long dining table offended him, decorated with so many candles and empty plates, but so little food.

At the far end of the room, O'Toole ate a sparse supper. He politely wiped his mouth with a napkin, beckoning his attendant forward. "You have been exceedingly quiet today. I don't think I've heard from you or Mammon since yesterday." He gestured to a plate questioningly.

"Thank you, sir, but no. I'd rather have a full meal, not a mouse's scavenge of food."

"Suit yourself. How goes the pursuit?"

"Well, my lord. Mammon was making a visit down himself to see how things were going. From his source, LaCrucis and his Hollow Men were tight on Vix's tail."

"All very good. The girl and Tom Vix. Have them brought to me personally."

Mr. Zeb frowned. He had foreseen O'Toole wanting

to punish Tom Vix personally, but the girl? "My lord?"

O'Toole looked up from his dinner slowly, a cloud forming on his brow.

"I do not understand. What could you possibly need the girl for?"

"I did not ask you to understand my commands, Zeb."

Mr. Zeb bowed low, hiding well the broil inside. "I'll contact Mammon right away, my lord."

Industrial's bamboo gardens were nothing to blink at. The stalks were strong enough, handling the district's noxious air, but the other plants, grass walkways, and fountains were all decrepit and run down. Few of the gardens that lined the wall around Industrial were tended very well. With the low air quality and the haze, as well as the higher percentage of acid rain, the upkeep was as constant as it was unrewarding.

That being said, living near the gardens was still highly sought after. The bamboo did its trick, providing cleaner air than around the factories, and so only those who had their run of Industrial's streets were able to afford the real estate.

The small figure's eyes scanned beyond the bamboo, looking for the place that had been described to him. He only wondered how Allwurst, a lowly thief, could have gotten a place to live here, of all places.

Thinking a little more on it, it did make sense. Allwurst was hated, but respected. Everyone knew he was good at his job—whatever job he was being hired for at that given moment.

There it was.

A ramshackle thing if I'd ever seen.

The great wall that surrounded Limbo towered behind this small house. The figure hesitated to call it a house. It seemed more like a tool shed with reinforced doors and barred windows. Looking around for witnesses, the cloaked figure slipped forward, reaching into his coat and pulling out a sleepy automaton. It was slender and segmented, but no bigger than a rat.

"Get me in," he whispered, and the automaton slunk

to the ground, flattening itself to fit under the door.

Scratching was heard inside for a moment, then the satisfying sounds of mechanisms sliding into their slots. The figure nodded, impressed, hearing — not one, not two, not three, but — four locks release. Then, nothing.

If Allwurst was paranoid enough to have four locks, perhaps he had also set traps? Gingerly, the small figure reached forward, ever so slowly twisting the handle to listen for more clicks. Knob fully rotated, the door swung inward freely.

"What a pigsty." *And that's saying something from me. I use a trash bin as a desk and it isn't this dirty.*

Allwurt's one-room abode was a topsy-turvy affair. Cheap metal mugs were left everywhere, some overturned with their contents having long dried out over the victimized tables and floors. Dirty clothes lay strewn over the bed, which had no sheets and a single soiled pillow; and tossed across the room's single chair, which sat awkwardly alone in the middle of the room. The whole place smelled of must and armpits.

The small figure, George, stepped in and closed the

door, lighting up a small lantern he carried with him. The automaton raised its head from a nearby table, wagging its metal tail.

"Yes, yes, very good. Now help me find the other door, will you?"

He shivered as the thing plopped to the ground, its flat head scanning the floor in waves. George knew well that automatons were not Hollow Men, but they still gave him the creeps. If he hadn't been given this automaton for the job, George would have been forced to figure all this out on his own. He would've been perfectly fine with that.

In little time, the wormlike automaton raised its head again, then slapping it down on a cheap rug.

"Oh, of all the clichés." George crossed the room, throwing the rug back and regretting the cloud of sand and dirt it released into the air. "Allwurst, I expected something a little more clever from you. Guess I shouldn't have."

He bent down, fiddling with the trapdoor built into the dirt floor. Locked, of course. George looked over his shoulder. "A little help?"

The automaton excitedly scurried into the crack, finding the mechanism and turning it. He threw the trapdoor open, finding the automaton inside, sitting on top of a large satchel bag. Some other loot sat underneath, unorganized as the rest of Allwurst's house. The worm wagged its tail end happily.

"Thanks. I could have figured it out, you know. But we're pressed for time."

George picked up the little automaton and set him to the side, taking the bamboo canisters from his oversized coat. Gently — focusing so his hands did not shake — he connected the wires between the explosives and set the rigging. He was careful not to slam the trap door down. "Shame, all those gold cards going to waste like that. Right. Time to go!"

Explosives rigged, George quickly got up, covering the trapdoor with the rug. He scooped up the automaton and left, waiting for it to lock the front door. The night was quiet, warmer than usual. He passed through a multileveled junkyard that dwarfed the line of bamboo trees next to it, ducking under some large swinging crane hooks. The other districts would always find ways to pile their trash on Industrial, even when there was no more room.

Gradually, the passing bamboo gardens became nicer, finally becoming decorated with running streams and fountains, colorful flowers and burning lamps. He'd passed into the Arts District, and George drew in a deep breath of the clean air. He snuck into the trees to pass a lounging couple. With his dirty attire, he couldn't afford to be seen here.

Picking his way through the trees, he found the garden he was looking for. Ash sat sipping tea, talking with one of her girls, and looking relaxed. He could tell by the girl's posture, though, it was a serious conversation.

George checked the surroundings before leaving the cover of the trees, strolling up behind Ash.

"Good evening, George," said Ash without turning around.

Ash's eyes were sharper than they used to be, and she was dressed in garments more simple than he brothel owner's attire, a powder blue button down dress with indigo highlights and loose sleeves. A pendant hung from her neck, depicting a roaring lion. In this new modesty she was, if anything, more beautiful than before. Then again, perhaps it was the deadly look upon her face. To any passerby, she probably seemed to simply be enjoying tea with a friend. George knew her better, though—she was angry, and she was plotting.

He came around to sit with them. "Ma'am. Jazz."

"Hey, Georgie," Jasmine said with a big smile.

"It's just George, please." He took the automaton from his pocket, extending the sleeping worm to Ash. "Job's done."

Ash took the automaton, letting it sleep on her armrest. "Thank you. I would tell you to keep him, but I know how you feel about automatons and homunculi. Here, take these in its stead." She held out a thick stack of gold cards.

George whistled low. His quick eyes told him the stack was high over ten gold cards. "That's too much, ma'am."

"Then you'll have too much. I want you to take it. Give some to people who need your help, if you wish."

"Fair enough. Thank you. May I ask a question?"
She waited.

"Why have me trap his stash? Why not take the gold

cards that were there, if you were just trying to get rid of Allwurst?"

She smiled pertly, a dark look in her eyes. "I have no worries of getting rid of anyone. I'm simply creating a distraction."

"There's something I want to tell you."

Kit looked up, surprised. Mr. Tom had been silent and surly, leading the Den for the past two hours on their trek. "What is it?" Her voice was soft from the previous extended silence.

"I'm sorry."

She raised her eyebrows in shock. "You're apologizing. You don't ever—wait, what are you sorry for?"

"Don't make a thing of it, girl. For before. Emily." He sighed deeply, as if he'd carried the weight of that apology since she'd left years ago.

"Well, you were right. I should have listened to you back then. I dragged her up to Limbo."

There was a soft hurt that lingered between them. It wasn't the usual bitterness, nor was it anger, but a sad regret. Kit wondered what her life would have been like if they'd had this conversation sooner.

"I know growing up under Limbo wasn't always the easiest life."

"You wanted to save us. I get it. And I never blamed you for that. You did a lot of good. Saved a lot of orphans from a worse fate."

"I tried. I didn't always succeed. I pushed away the person that meant the most to me in this world." He looked at her sadly.

Kit held back the moisture in her eyes, throat tightening. "Like you said, it wasn't the easiest life. Things don't always turn out like they should. They get all bricked up." A single tear slipped onto her cheek.

Mr. Tom stopped walking, grabbed Kit and pulled her into a big hug. "That was no excuse for me to let you just walk away. You're my . . ." He struggled with the words as members of the Den passed by, gawking, but trying not to. "You're like a daughter to me, Kit. I'm sorry for letting you survive on your own for so long. Please always remember, I love you dearly."

Slowly, she hugged him back. She had waited forever to hear those words. Growing up without parents, Mr. Tom had been her guardian, her protector, and her father figure. But it had always been unspoken.

"And now you're going to go through that hole and leave Limbo," he said, voice growing hoarse.

"Come with us!"

"Lukos' appearance here has changed things. There's a fight that I must return to."

She sunk back, looking at the ground and nodding.

"Promise me, Kit. You two will survive."

"Of course."

She looked up and was surprised to see that his eyes had grown dark, full of an old anger. He nodded, gave her a pained smile, and hugged her once more before turning away, tapping his stick against the ground twice and limping back toward the front of the Den.

Kit stood still for a moment, her heart racing.

Why does that sound like goodbye?

Lukos was tired of walking. Tired of running. Just tired of everything really. Arm and hand were still sore from being cut up, and the saber at his side, while invigorating, had only added to the weight and inconvenience he carried toward their goal.

The cavernous underworld had started to change again. It was lighter here, and it was growing colder. Some sort of light must be filtering down from Limbo, or so Lukos thought. And a strange smell was in the air. Something bitter, yet tangy and refreshing. Like salt, but pungent.

Pan walked beside him, quiet, solemn. He still blamed himself for the staircase, Lukos knew.

"How much longer until we reach the hole?" Lukos asked. He didn't much care, but was trying to spark up some sort of conversation. The two hadn't hit it off very well at first, but Lukos had grown to like Pan. Without many friends in the world, Lukos felt like he was about to lose one in leaving.

"The hole?" Pan looked up without emotion. "We're here. Listen, you can hear the ocean."

Lukos listened. That sound that Lukos had mistaken for some as-of-yet unseen windy tunnels became more distinct as they walked along. It was rushing, but it was inconsistent.

No, that's not right. It's quite consistent. Coming in . . . waves.

Ahead of them, their companions began to disappear over a slope. Lukos noticed a sliver of pale light touching them before they disappeared. Eagerly, he picked up the pace to follow.

He reached the slope, softly descending into another chamber. The sudden brightness blinded him at first, his eyes having adjusted to the underworld.

No, he thought, remembering something he had read in Doyle's library once. *This is a cave. This is called a cave. And those . . .*

He laughed to himself. That sound. The reason it sounded like waves was because *they were* waves. Water splashed high over a sharp bank of rocks and pebbles, foaming as it settled back again.

The ocean. Salt water. That's why it smells so strange. He took it all in with amazement. It looked so natural and so . . . *real.* Nothing manufactured or created by artisans, but something that existed without the hand of an alchemist or architect.

Down below, Pan called out. "You all right Lukos?"

Lukos ran down, nearly stumbling before he remembered that he was on a slope. "Yes. I'm sorry, it's just so different."

Some of the life returned to Pan's eyes. "Yes, yes it is. It's amazing. I remember the first time I saw it. I'm a little envious, to be honest. Maybe one day I'll come find the two of you out there. Follow in your footsteps."

As they spoke, some excitement started near the waterline.

Pan's breath slipped out between his lips. "Just in time."

A ship drifted in on the waves. Nothing big or glamorous—the sides of the ship blackened and the sail short but wide—but to Lukos it was astounding. There really were people left in the world outside Limbo. Rugged and weathered men on board jumped from the boat in thick rubber suits, pulling the ship to shore and setting up a wooden ramp for passage.

A burly man with a shaved head and many tattoos stomped off the ship, arms wide in greeting. "Tom Vix, you old bastard! You look rough as ever. Skies above, you look worse, actually."

"The last few days have been hell," Mr. Tom answered simply. "I need a favor, Ulrich."

"*Oof*, a favor. You know I'm a busy man."

A single, horrible cry came from behind them, sounding neither beast nor human — like the new Hollow Men that Lukos fought. A visible shift in the atmosphere set in, the children beginning to weep and shake. The smugglers tensed, and Ulrich looked at Mr. Tom, serious now, and less friendly.

"What's going on, Vix?"

"I need you to take the children, and some passengers."

Ulrich stared at Mr. Tom for a moment before breaking out into belly laughter.

"Shut up, now is not the time! Hollow Men are on our tail. LaCrucis is coming!"

"LaCrucis? That old wives' tale you cave dwellers go on about, right?"

Mr. Tom grabbed the smuggler by his arms. "Get the children on board, Ulrich."

"Careful, oldtimer. Besides, you know I don't take passengers. Now where are your goods?"

Mr. Tom clenched his teeth. "They were destroyed by what follows us. If you don't take these children, they will die."

The man stood steadfast. "Not my problem, Vix."

Mr. Tom shook his head, turning around. "Pan. Lukos. Kit. Come here please, bring me your weapons."

The three joined them quickly, knowing they didn't have much time, and handed their weapons to Vix—the two swords taken from Hollows, and Pan's grappling gun. He in turn handed them to Ulrich. Then, Mr. Tom nodded to Vasi and Jimmerson. They rushed forward, grabbing Kit and Pan by the arms and binding them. Confused, Lukos reached out, his fists clenching, trying to decide whether to attack Jimmerson or not.

"Don't do it, boy!"

Lukos stopped cold, looking over his shoulder at Mr. Tom. Star clung to his leg, crying and pleading for them to stop.

The old thief's face was unreadable. "It's for my children, Lukos. You know as well as I do what the Hollows would do to them. If you can let them die to those savages, then go ahead and stop Jimmerson and Vasi. Otherwise play along."

Lukos looked around, torn, seeing the shocked and betrayed faces of Pan and Kit, the fear upon the children's eyes, and the shame washing over Vasi and Jimmerson. "What are you planning on doing?"

Mr. Tom turned to Ulrich. "Take the weapons. The swords are made out of infernium. Take these three as well. They are fit and young, and would make good slaves for the market. This one, especially, is unique. His arm is an infernium alloy, but not mechanical."

Ulrich looked Mr. Tom over. Even he looked shocked.

Another screech from above, this one closer. They could hear it now, the chaotic march of so many metal feet.

"While you're at it, take this, too." Mr. Tom looked

at his walking stick, rubbing the carved fox head, and tossed it to the man, who caught it deftly. "It's made from infernium, as well."

"You really are desperate, aren't you?" Ulrich looked to his smugglers. "You heard him. Get the kids on board, and these three." Ulrich studied Lukos with interest, a sort of greed in his eyes as he stared at his metal arm. "I'm assuming you want to come on board as well, then?"

The smugglers started boarding the children, some grabbing two or three of them to save time. The children of the Fox Den cried, not understanding what was transpiring around them. Their entire world had ended in a matter of days. Lukos was heartbroken—he should have never resisted the Hollows. The cost was too high.

"We're staying," Mr. Tom told the smuggler captain. "Don't bother coming back, this will be the last time we meet."

"You're just full of surprises, Vix, you know that? It was a pleasure doing business with you." He reached out a hand to shake, but Mr. Tom turned away. He looked straight at that tunnel opening, never looking again at

Kit or the others.

As for Kit, tears streamed down her face as she walked forward, escorted by smugglers. It was the only visible sign of her pain or despair. Lukos followed as she and Pan—struggling a bit more, but obviously defeated—were brought onto the ship. He looked back once more as Vasi and Jimmerson followed Vix. The three adults, all that remained of Limbo's underworld, stood side by side, facing the entrance, awaiting the coming horrors. A rough man with a beard covering all the way to his belly shoved Lukos forward, causing him to fall near the edge of the ship. Lukos watched as the water splashed against the ship, an inky quality clinging to the wood and the pebbles of the cave's coast as the waves fell back again.

"Stupid! Don't fall in the water!" said the bearded smuggler, dragging Lukos the last few feet until he was on the rough wooden deck. "We gotta sell you, don't want you dead."

The children were all forced to sit in the middle of the deck, while Pan, Kit, and Lukos were shackled and secured to the mast.

"Mind the choppy ride," Ulrich said to the three. "We don't usually carry people as goods, so I can't offer you any comfort."

Pan and Kit only glared at the man defiantly. Lukos slumped against the wood, exhausted and drained. He had no fight left to give.

"All right, let's get going. I don't care to stick around for whatever devils they have to worry about."

The men set to work, the two smugglers in thick rubber suits jumping back down to push the ship from the shore, and just as quickly the ship was drifting back to sea. Lukos couldn't believe it, staring, motionless upon the rocking vessel, as Mr. Tom and his followers stood with their backs turned.

Soon, they were out of the cave and into a world that was wide open. Lukos saw nothing on the bright gray horizon but water and rocks. He looked back to a giant cliff face, jutting high into the sky, where the shining walls of Limbo concealed the only world he'd ever known to exist.

He looked back at the horizon, wondering what kind of world lay beyond.

The winged lizard alternated between slithering and flying, clinging to walls and the uneven streets. Mammon followed it patiently. If he couldn't get everything he wanted immediately, at least the Fox Den had been destroyed. That band of rebels had been a grain of sand in their eye for too many years. Small, insignificant—*yes*—but an insult to everything they had accomplished.

He smiled. The grimy scar on Limbo that was Industrial always reminded him of his own fortune in this world. It was his constant motivation to accumulate more. His duty to sap from others.

It wasn't long before a certain dingy shack stood before him. Mammon reached for the door, felt the resistance of the locks, and pushed. He was surprised when it didn't give, impressed even. He put some effort into it.

The heavy door cracked inward, taking part of the frame with it and leaving chunks in the doorway. Mammon counted four deadlocks jutting out as it swung all the way open before taking in the small apartment.

"My, my. You really did need the money, didn't you?" He stepped into Allwurst's home, clucking his tongue at the mess. "For a man with a useful reputation . . ."

He stopped midsentence, scanning the room. His eyes landed over the ratty rug on the floor, laying crooked, out of place. Underneath, he found what he was looking for. Mammon's smile grew into a hungry grin as he reached for the trapdoor.

Take back what is mine.

He lifted the latch.

An otherwise quiet and relatively peaceful evening for the Industrial District was rocked by an explosion, consuming the silence. Allwurt's shack, and the surrounding bamboo, was sent up in flames.

"I'm sorry it came to this." Mr. Tom wrung his gloved hands together, missing his walking stick already.

Vasi gave the old thief a brief hug. "We would follow you to the end of the world."

"For us, this may very well be the end. I only hope they find a way out of their situation now." A sad look appeared on his face. "Kit will grow old hating me."

"She's a smart one, sir," said Jimmerson. "She'll figure out a way to survive. Pan, too. You did the right thing."

The sounds of the Hollows were loud now. It wouldn't be long.

"Thank you both. We had a good run, didn't we?"

LaCrucis crested the top of that hidden slope. He aimed his pistol and fired without hesitation, and Vasi fell back, her blood pouring over the pebbles. Mr. Tom and Jimmerson charged, but not for long.

The last thing Mr. Tom remembered seeing as his vision faded were two of those damnable humanoid Hollow Men bending down over him, their swords at the ready.

About The Author

C. Michael McGannon was born in Mannheim, Germany while his parents were serving abroad. As soon as his hand figured out what to do with a pencil, he was drawing wild monsters and eerily recognizable stick figures of his family, and as soon as he could string words together on paper, well . . . he's been crafting stories ever since.

He loves dragons, foxes, and sushi, and is a connoisseur of a well-timed, *the-cheesier-the-better pun*. His free time is spent enjoying family and friends, gaming, and engaged in the deep study of folklore and mythology from around the world. As much as possible, Michael enjoys traveling to fan conventions, meeting readers face to face, and sharing adventures from his own love of storytelling.

McGannon is the co-author of the best-selling fantasy

series for young adults, *Charlie Sullivan and the Monster Hunters (Wyvern's Peak Publishing)*; a collection of dark fiction stories for adults, *KAOS Obsidere: The Nightmare Has Begun (Dark Waters Press)*; and a collection of original stories about Japanese yokai titled, *Yokai Tales: Stories From Japan's Grand and Mysterious Traditions of Folklore (Incendia Books)*, in addition to the *Hollow World* series.

He is also co-host of The Monster Guys Podcast, the Yokai Podcast, and Faerie Tales Podcast—weekly conversations exploring interests in folklore, mythology, and storytelling from countries and tribes the world over.

Visit C. Michael McGannon at *www.TheMonsterGuys.com*, or at *www.Facebook.com/cmichaelmcgannon*, or *www.Twitter.com/MichaelMcGannon*.